*A Candlelight
Ecstasy Romance*®

"TRUST ME," LOGAN MURMURED. "THAT'S ALL I ASK OF YOU."

"I can't *ever* trust you," Danella answered, nearly choking on the words. "I've seen what loving you can do to a woman. If not for you, Jackie Wesson would still be alive. You killed her when you left her, Logan. I'm never going to let you hurt me as much as you hurt her."

"After all this time, you still believe those lies about me?" Logan groaned.

"It's your word against hers," Danella said defensively.

"That's right," he concurred, his expression turning icy. "And it's time you decided once and for all which one of us you really believe."

LOVING PERSUASION

Emma Bennett

A CANDLELIGHT ECSTASY ROMANCE

CANDLELIGHT ECSTASY ROMANCES

Published by
Dell Publishing Co., Inc.
1 Dag Hammarskjold Plaza
New York, New York 10017

Dell ® TM 681510, Dell Publishing Co., Inc.

Candlelight Ecstasy Romance®, 1,203,540, is a
registered trademark of Dell Publishing Co., Inc.
New York, New York.

ISBN: 0-440-15113-9

Printed in the United States of America

First printing—April 1985

To Our Readers:

We have been delighted with your enthusiastic response to Candlelight Ecstasy Romances®, and we thank you for the interest you have shown in this exciting series.

In the upcoming months we will continue to present the distinctive sensuous love stories you have come to expect only from Ecstasy. We look forward to bringing you many more books from your favorite authors and also the very finest work from new authors of contemporary romantic fiction.

As always, we are striving to present the unique, absorbing love stories that you enjoy most—books that are more than ordinary romance. Your suggestions and comments are always welcome. Please write to us at the address below.

Sincerely,

The Editors
Candlelight Romances
1 Dag Hammarskjold Plaza
New York, New York 10017

CHAPTER ONE

"Dan Jones, please check in at the front desk."

As Logan Spencer listened to the mechanical-sounding voice of the page, he lounged indolently at the front desk of the Wilmington Hilton Inn. He could wait to talk to Jones until morning, he thought, but he didn't want to. Although tired after his quick trip to Raleigh, he was too restless to call it a night, and after checking in at his office and reading his secretary's notes, he wanted to know more about Blaketon Pharmaceuticals. His secretary, Justine's brief description, in addition to what he'd been hearing and reading in the news, had whetted his interest.

Blake Company and its acquisition by Warrington was an issue that concerned people thereabouts. The company was the economic vitality of Blaketon, virtually feeding the entire community. And anything that concerned Blaketon directly or indirectly affected Wilmington. Public sentiment strongly opposed Liston Blake, ex-president, for his mismanagément, and the community was relieved but wary when Warrington had announced their takeover of the faltering company.

Logan was curious about Dan Jones. Despite his previous dealings with Blake Company, the name was unfamiliar to him. He wondered who Jones was. What role did he play in the new order? There was only one way to get his questions answered, Logan thought: He would have a talk with the man. He had that deep-down feeling that he was going to take the account. It might prove interesting being their public relations expert. He had always enjoyed working with Horace Warrington in the past, and he saw no reason why this time should be an exception. And this might prove to be a challenging assignment, the kind that made the boring ones bearable. However, he wanted to get the blanks filled in before he made his final judgment.

One could never have told by Logan's nonchalant bearing that he was anxiously awaiting anyone there. Quite casually he lifted a hand, running it through his thick, sandy brown hair, which was neatly combed away from his face, except for one thatch that defied the orderly style, falling across his forehead in a rebellious wave. Then he dropped his hand to his face, rubbing his index and middle fingers over the bridge of his nose.

He was a striking man, a man most women found very attractive. The chiseled contour of his face was softened by his pleasant expression; his lips curved into a teasing smile; and his sapphire-blue eyes twinkled with vibrant energy. Even his broken nose added to his aura of ruggedness. He was the type of man who didn't have to speak in order for people to be aware of him; his very presence commanded attention.

His clothes, custom-made, were tailored for his broad frame, and they were well coordinated for fit and color, enhancing his masculinity. His navy blue sport jacket smoothly caressed his shoulders; his tan slacks accented his thick, muscular thighs; and the light blue shirt

10

nearly matched the color of his eyes. An ecru pullover sweater completed the casual, sturdy look.

Again the mechanical tones flowed through the lobby of the hotel. "Dan Jones, please check in at the front desk."

After a few more minutes of waiting and not receiving any response, Logan looked at his wristwatch, unconsciously sighing in disappointment; then he turned his head toward the desk clerk. "Thanks. I guess he's not here." He took out his business card, picked up a pen, and wrote his home phone number on the back. "If you don't mind, give this to him and tell him to call me as soon as he gets in." When the clerk took the card, Logan turned, walking away.

Just at that moment a woman opened the door and entered the lobby, a gust of wind blowing in with her. Her face had a natural, healthy sheen; her cheeks and lips were brushed a deep rose color by the autumn briskness; her brown hair was wind-blown. She wore a pair of fully lined white pleated trousers, a yellow turtleneck sweater, and a creamy three-quarter-length jacket. She was carrying two large shopping bags.

Logan, now striding out of the hotel and moving in the woman's direction, was totally enthralled by this windswept creature. He was looking where he was going, and he was watching where she was going, but she was doing neither. With a heavy thud that he could have easily avoided if he had so desired, he allowed her to bump into the hard wall of his chest.

"Oh, I'm sorry," they both murmured at the same time, dropping to their knees to retrieve the packages that she had dropped.

"I didn't see you," she said, her words rushing past her lips, her mind clearly on other matters. "I'm afraid I'm in a hurry." She distractedly excused herself, lifting her face at the same time Logan did, their heads collid-

11

ing with a dull thud. Again she murmured impatiently, pulling away from him, "Oh, I'm so sorry."

"Quite all right." Logan's dry retort hinted at suppressed laughter. "I enjoy bumping heads with beautiful women." If she heard his comment, she ignored him, her eyes darting furtively around the lobby as her hands wildly grabbed for the contents of her bag. "Here," he announced, picking up the last package, handing it to her, and letting her stand up before he did. "I think this is it."

As he dropped the small box into her bag she briefly glanced at his face. Although her eyes were on him, they never brought him into focus. "Thanks," she mumbled, sidestepping him. She cast an apologetic smile over her shoulder as she hurried away, but it was obvious to Logan that she had never really noticed him.

"It's quite all right," Logan called softly after her retreating figure, his words dying into silence. "I love bumping into beautiful women who never see me." He chuckled to himself. "More than that, I love being ignored."

But even then he didn't immediately walk away. He stood for several seconds with his hand on the door, looking over his shoulder, watching her as she scurried to the front desk. He knew that she hadn't been too impressed with him, but he had definitely been impressed with her. She was an attractive woman. Just the kind he could go for.

Her brown hair, highlighted with red, was short and straight, slightly turning under at the ends, with an illusion of bangs wisping across her forehead. Her eyes, he had noticed in that quick glance, were an unusual color, raw umber, a beautiful golden brown that was spiked with gray highlights. Her makeup was minimal but he thought, with a complexion like hers and with that smile, it wasn't essential.

He shrugged his shoulders and turned, moving out

the doors into the cold October evening, the wind blowing through his hair, whipping it against his face. He hunched his shoulders against the cold and walked toward the parking lot. He'd done all he could to locate Dan Jones; he'd left his name and home phone number. Maybe the fellow would call him when he got in that night or in the morning. But if Jones didn't call by morning, Logan decided, he would try to reach him again.

He hadn't walked very far when he thought he heard his name carried by the wind. He stopped walking and listened. It could have been his imagination.

"Mr. Spencer."

No, it wasn't his imagination: He did hear it. He turned, waiting, watching the woman in the white slacks and coat as she raced down the street toward him, shopping bags still under her arms.

When she stood directly in front of him, breathing deeply, her short hair blowing across her face as the wind swirled around them, she said, "I'm terribly sorry about bumping into you."

Logan chuckled softly, dropping his hands on his hips in an indolent athletic stance, shaking his head in puzzled surprise. "You mean to tell me that you ran all the way out here just to apologize?" Even if she had, he thought fleetingly, he was glad.

She raised a hand to push wisps of hair out of her mouth and eyes. "No, I didn't." Her eyes were as cold as the wind that blew about them. She held his card up. "The clerk at the desk said you wanted to see Dan Jones."

He had never felt disappointment as acutely as he felt it when he heard her flat announcement. Could she be married to Jones? "Yes," he said, "Dan Jones of Blaketon Pharmaceuticals?"

She nodded her head, seeing an unaccountable flicker of disappointment in his eyes. "I think I'm the Dan

13

Jones whom you were looking for." There was that infinitesimal pause before she said, "Danella C. Jones, Blaketon Pharmaceuticals, Blaketon, North Carolina."

Comprehension dawned and Logan smiled. "Danella." The murmured word was lost in the blast of wind. "Of course! My secretary probably abbreviated your name to Dan."

Again he chuckled to himself, the laughter reaching his lips and his eyes. He reached out, taking the shopping bags from Danella's arms, easily lodging them under one of his. With his free hand he guided her toward the hotel.

"Come on. Let's get out of this weather," he said, and in the next breath he added, "Have you eaten?"

She hadn't, but she decided not to let him know that. "I got a bite in the mall," she said slightly coldly. Her eyes inadvertently went to her bundles. "I was doing some early Christmas shopping, since I was in town."

His eyes appreciatively examined her slender figure. "A second bite wouldn't hurt you any." He grinned in a most beguiling manner. "How about our discussing Blaketon Pharmaceuticals over dinner?"

Danella shook her head and opened her mouth to protest. Before she could utter the words, however, Logan spoke again.

"I just returned from Raleigh, and I haven't had a chance to eat, and I'm starved."

Danella could understand that, her eyes running his full length and breadth. He was a powerful man, and she remembered Jackie's telling her how much Logan enjoyed eating. Odd, she thought, she knew so much about him; yet, she had never seen him. Therefore she wouldn't have recognized him when she bumped into him.

When Danella didn't speak immediately, Logan's lips curved into a whimsical smile. "Please don't say no. I don't like eating alone."

Now that Danella had met him, she could understand her friend's falling in love with Logan. He was that kind of man, and he knew it. He knew he attracted female attention; he knew his power with women. And, Danella reminded herself, he would be one to capitalize on it.

The thought of having dinner with Logan was not appealing at all to Danella, but she knew she had to speak to him sometime. "I'll just run upstairs and leave these," she said, taking the bags from him as they walked into the lobby. "I'll be right back."

Logan watched as she bustled out of sight, soon lost behind the gliding metal doors. He walked around for a while, finally settling his large frame on one of the occasional chairs. In the meantime Danella ran to her room and laid the packages on her dresser. Taking the necessary time, she combed her wind-blown hair and reapplied her makeup, daubing on more of her favorite perfume. Before she thought about it, she almost took the time to slip out of her boots and put on a pair of beautiful high heels.

But when she realized what she was doing, she stopped. She slowly dropped her dainty shoes back into their box and replaced the lid. Her meeting with Logan Spencer was entirely business, and there was no place in their association for anything more, not even the suggestion of more. Sitting on the edge of the bed, holding the box in her lap, Danella was inundated with memories. As vividly as if it were that day five years earlier, she remembered walking into the intensive-care unit. She could still see Jackie's face; she could still hear her heart-rending cries for Logan.

Because Danella had been working in the Chicago office when Jackie had met and had dated Logan, Danella had never met him personally. But Jackie had spent hours on the phone, telling her about what a wonderful man he was, and she had written Danella long letters, confiding the intimacy of their affair. Then had come that fateful phone call, and a distraught Jackie had poured out the agony of her soul. Logan had left her after callously ending their relationship.

So Danella felt that her distaste for the man was justified. If Jackie had been a weak person, Danella could have understood; she would have made allowances. But Jackie hadn't been weak. She had been a strong woman. Still, Logan Spencer's effect on her had been even stronger. Jackie had never been able to accept the ending of her relationship with him and to face the reality of everyday living.

Danella couldn't forget the depressed person Jackie became. She would never forget the months that she had listened as the distraught woman poured out the longings and sorrows of her heart, all of it caused by Logan Spencer. Even if she forgot everything else, Danella would never forget the anguish she had felt when she had stood in the intensive-care unit, watching Jackie die, listening to her delirious cry for Logan. She would never forget that moment. Because of Jackie, Danella could muster up nothing but loathing and contempt for Logan.

And if it had not been for Horace Warrington's insisting on hiring Logan Spencer's firm to handle the public relations for Blaketon Pharmaceuticals, Danella would have refused. But one could hardly refuse the president of the company, she thought, standing and laying the shoe box on the bed. And one could hardly argue with the statistics that proved that Logan Spencer was one of the best public relations consultants on the East Coast.

If she must work with him, she must. But it would be purely a professional relationship. She looked at the shoes, grinned, and waved at them, slinging her purse over her shoulder and briskly walking out of the room, down the hall, and to the elevator. When she arrived in the lobby, she straightened her shoulders, and moved toward Logan, who stood and began walking to meet her. When he was beside her, he cupped her bent elbow with his hand. His touch bothered Danella with its proprietorial firmness and authority. She carefully but pointedly disengaged her arm, making only a half-hearted effort to enjoy his easy conversation as they made their way into the luxurious restaurant.

After they had ordered their dinner and were sitting comfortably with their drinks, listening to the soft music of the local band, Logan continued to talk, trying to get her to relax. He seemed to be in no hurry to broach the subject of Blaketon Pharmaceuticals and seemed to Danella to be thoroughly enjoying the evening.

"Tell me something about yourself," he suggested softly, lifting his glass of Scotch and water to his lips.

Danella pulled her gaze from the band, leveling it at Logan. "Is this personal interest or is it in the line of duty?" she inquired rather coldly.

"In the line of duty, ma'am," he intoned, his lips curving into a smile. "But I'll cross-reference anything you tell me so I can use it personally if ever there should be a time and place for that." He waited for her reply, the blue eyes studying her.

"I doubt there will be a time or a place for that, Mr. Spencer."

She could see that Logan Spencer was already entertaining ideas of having more than a business relationship with her. The very thought of it infuriated her. Well, he'd better set his sights on someone else, she thought. She couldn't afford the kind of regrets that Logan Spencer left behind. She curled her fingers around the stem of her glass. "I'm here to work. I came to Wilmington because I need a good PR person." Her face was as cool and collected as her words. "I want to hire you to promote Blaketon Pharmaceuticals. That's my only interest in you." She paused for dramatic effect, lowered her face, and sipped her drink. Then she set

17

the glass down and lifted her eyes to his. "My personal life is full and complete, and I find that I can take care of it quite well without consultation."

Logan's amusement was as annoying as it was evident. "Then, Ms. Jones, since I have been properly shot out of the saddle, I suggest that we turn our conversation to business matters." Like her, he paused affectively, lifting his glass and slowly turning it around, his blue eyes following the swirl of the amber-colored liquid. "However, I assure you that on a personal level I'm quite delightful and just as reliable."

"Mr. Spencer," she answered, trying to sound as haughty as she could, "I have no doubt as to your qualifications"—she didn't try to soften her blow—"but I'm really not interested in a mass-market lover. I'm much more selective than that."

Logan made no retort, but his eyes turned icy blue with anger. He didn't respond to her for a moment, stunned by her curt response to his innocent comment. She was an odd woman, this Danella Jones, he thought. She definitely appealed to him, and the longer he was around her, the more he found his initial spark of interest in Blaketon Pharmaceuticals fanning into a consuming desire to know more about Danella Jones personally. The dual challenge of launching Blaketon Pharmaceuticals and of breaking Danella's cold reserve set his adrenaline flowing. Mass-market lover, was he? He'd show her!

After their dinner was served, the food lauded, and the compliments to the chef extended, Logan channeled their conversation toward business, asking for an extensive rundown on Danella and Blaketon Pharmaceuticals. He wanted to know more than what she had told Justine earlier in the day.

"Ms. Jones"—he lifted his face, taking his eyes off his food and grinning across the table at her—"may I please call you something besides Ms. Jones?" When

Danella's expression showed her disapproval, he quickly said mockingly, "Purely in the interest of expedience, Ms. Jones. Nothing personal meant."

"Danella, then," she responded.

"I'll settle for that." he said, and then, as if testing the waters, went on. "But I've got a feeling that you're not really a Danella all the time." He hesitated. "And I know you're not a Dan. I suspect, Ms. Jones, that you're a Danny." He crossed his forearms on the table and leaned on them. "May I call you Danny?"

"I'd prefer that you didn't," she returned stonily. "I don't allow anyone but my parents to call me Danny."

Logan inclined his head slightly and shrugged. Danella's aversion to him was obvious, but he couldn't understand it. "I prefer to be called Logan. Helps when you're dealing with the public if you and your client are on a first-name basis." He looked at her steadily. "And again, that's purely good business, Ms. Danella Jones."

"I'm all for good business," Danny quipped, "but unlike you, I think a certain amount of formality makes for better business."

Logan, choosing to ignore her charge, gently teased, "I think you're a Danny." He tasted her name, holding it on his tongue a long time, savoring its full essence. "I like it; it seems to fit you." Then, before she could censure him or direct him back on course, he said, "Okay, Miss Jones, tell me all about yourself and Blaketon and your mutual association." He leaned back in his chair, his eyes dark and speculative, ready to listen. "And you can begin by telling me why, when you apparently don't care for me, you chose my firm to handle your publicity."

Danella straightened her shoulders and leaned back in her chair. Then she sipped her wine, gazing out the window at the beautiful Cape Fear River, its peaceful waters reflecting the bright lights of the hotel and the buildings along the wharf. She turned her head and gazed solemnly at him. "Actually, Logan, *I* didn't choose your firm. You were chosen for me by Warrington Corporation, our parent company."

Logan nodded, not reacting to her confession. "I've worked for them often through the years."

"And you've evidently impressed Mr. Warrington." Danny's straightforward look never wavered from Logan's face, which was shadowed by the dim light of the flickering candle. "He told me I would have the best public relations person in the country."

"And you got me," Logan said with satisfaction. "I've got a feeling that you aren't as impressed with my track record as Horace is."

"It doesn't matter what I think, Logan. You're the man whom Mr. Warrington has chosen, so you're the man with the job." She placed the fingers of each hand on the opposite wrist and pushed the bulky sleeves of her sweater up her arms. She discussed her opinions quite candidly, unconcerned with Logan's reaction. "I've learned during the years I've been with the company that Mr. Warrington generally knows what he's doing."

Danny was a puzzle to Logan. He couldn't figure her out at all. She seemed to extend the barest professional courtesy and nothing more; she was allowing none of herself to shine through. He could feel the chill wind of her reserve and distrust, but he still couldn't understand the reason for it.

"How long have you been with them?"

Again her answer was cool and professional, her tone methodical, as if she were answering questions in a personnel interview. "I've been with Warrington for eight years. I went to work for them right after graduating from college."

"About twenty-nine?"

She nodded. "I began in sales, working my way up. This summer Warrington bought Blake Company, which was on the verge of bankruptcy. We've changed the name to Blaketon Pharmaceuticals and are going to turn the company around while expanding into other areas."

"And what role do you play in the saving of this foundling?" Logan's tone was brisk, almost abrasive. "If Blake couldn't make it go, what makes Warrington think you can?"

Danny didn't resent his question. She was accustomed in her line of work to dealing with queries much more direct and accusatory than this. When she answered, her words were not a defense; they were a recitation of her qualifications, which stood her proud with Horace Warrington.

"Blake went under because of poor management and the fact that they were only a supplier. When we open the plant again at the end of this month, we're going to be a manufacturer *as well as* a supplier." Her eyes began to glow as she discussed her work. "You see, I'm a managerial and development consultant, so I'm qualified to salvage companies like Blake. And although I've never yet pulled a defunct company out of the hole, I've pulled some of our branch offices out of the red."

"What's the setup?

"Warrington is furnishing all the financial backing, and I'm furnishing the managerial know-how. We're asking you to furnish the publicity." Shadows flickered across her face in the candlelight. "Your job is to get our name and products before the public." She paused, then asked, "Are you interested?" Her gaze was as direct as her question.

Logan shifted his weight in the chair, leaned back, and looked squarely across the table at Danny. "I'm interested, but I can't perform a miracle by myself. It's going to take more than publicity, Danella. All the coverage in the world won't sell your products until you back them up. Ultimately you're the one to establish people's faith in Blaketon."

"There's no reason why we shouldn't succeed, then. I plan to do my job."

"Am I a liaison just for Blaketon or for you too?"

"Both, if it should prove necessary," Danella instantly responded. "Does that make a difference in your accepting the job?" At this point she would have been relieved for Logan to turn the job down.

"Not really. Just wondered where I stood so I can start planning."

"Probably your greatest concern will be the company." Danella smiled self-confidently. "I can take care of myself."

"I'm sure you think you can," Logan agreed, "but you're facing a different world when you're dealing with the press and public opinion." He lifted a thick brow. "I definitely want them on our side."

"And you think I don't."

"I don't know what you think," he retorted coolly. "But from now on you'll have to be very careful and let me handle all your public releases. You'll have to be cautious about handing out your opinions prematurely. People can construe what you say to mean anything they wish."

Danella sighed in irritation, but she acknowledged with a curt nod of her head.

"What's your position with the company?" Logan asked.

"I'm the manager," she replied in precise tones.

"According to the news, you kept a Blake on your payroll."

"That was one of the conditions of the takeover."

"Whom did you keep?"

"Lethia, a distant cousin to the former president. Know her?"

"I've heard of her," he replied. "She should be a good choice. The people of Blaketon seem to admire and respect her, which is more than they did Liston

Blake. She's still living in the main house of the plantation, isn't she?" Danny nodded; then Logan asked, "What's her position?"

"Assistant manager."

He whistled. "Quite a comedown." He eyed the waiter and signaled for their check. "Have you moved to Blaketon yet?"

"Next weekend. I'm staying here at the hotel until I can get all the details arranged—my house in Blaketon and you as public relations consultant." She grimaced as she remembered the crate-cluttered apartment she had left behind in Atlanta and the house she had to get ready in Blaketon before she could leave the hotel. "In fact, you've just reminded me of what's ahead."

"Moving is rough, huh?"

"No, to be honest, moving isn't the bad part at all." His face expressed his question. "It's the packing and the unpacking that's the problem. It's getting my house in Blaketon cleaned, painted, and ready for habitation that's rough."

"That's not what I had in mind," he pointed out. "Have you given much thought to what else you're facing?"

Danny heard kindness in his voice that she couldn't associate with the Logan Spencer of her memory, a special kindness that had nothing to do with Jackie Wesson's Logan Spencer. She felt the need to put distance between her and him. She reminded herself of his tactics and strategies; she knew he was not a man to be trusted.

"You know, those people in Blaketon are as closely knit together as a family." There was genuine compassion in his voice, and he wondered how this woman would fare when she came up against the people of a tightly knit rural community.

Wishing she misunderstood Logan, Danny stared at him a long time before she nodded her head. "I do

23

now. I really hadn't thought that much about it until I started looking for a place to live." She shrugged, remembering the snide remarks, the censurious looks. "I realized then that the people of this community resented my coming. It's not just that they resent Warrington's taking over; they resent me personally. Many of them feel that Lethia Blake should have been made manager."

"They would," Logan affirmed. "Blaketon is a small community built around the Blake family. And to them, Lethia is the benevolent matriarch. Anything that affects her affects them. Rather than hailing you as their savior, they probably feel like you're the enemy come to destroy them."

"That's about it. I've got to prove myself to the community, to the Blake employees, to the suppliers, and to the public." She winced. "Can you believe it?"

Logan reached across the table and laid his hand over hers in what was meant to be a reassuring gesture, but he noticed that Danella flinched from his touch. "That's something you don't have to worry about now. That's why you're hiring me."

Slowly Danella pulled her hand out from under his. She intended to set Logan Spencer straight right now. "That's why *Warrington* is hiring you." Her words reflected perfectly her disapproval over Warrington's choice.

Logan's eyes narrowed. Danella couldn't tell what he was thinking, but she saw him press his lips together. She figured that he was irritated.

"Are you ready to go?" His words were clipped, clearly indicating his annoyance.

When she nodded, he moved to her side of the table. As she stood, her back to his chest, he held her jacket for her, allowing her to slip her arms into the sleeves. His hands, holding the soft material, brushed against her neck. So intense was her dislike for the man that

24

she shivered. She couldn't stand to have him touch her. She quickly glanced up at Logan to see if he had noticed.

He had. "Cold, Danella?" She nodded and pulled her coat closely around herself. Accepting but not believing her answer, Logan changed the subject, asking, "What does Blaketon Pharmaceuticals mean to you?" They walked out of the restaurant, leisurely ambling through the lobby, headed nowhere in particular.

"Naturally a promotion," Danny replied, not minding his prying as long as they were discussing her job. "And a challenge. I want to prove to myself and to Mr. Warrington that I can do it. But mostly I have a desire to see the company prosper for the community once again."

"Altruistic?"

She shrugged, not knowing if he was needling her but not really concerned about it. "I like Blaketon. And I wouldn't mind spending the rest of my life there. As a member of the community, I'm concerned about Blaketon Pharmaceuticals."

"It may be better for you to live here in Wilmington and to commute to work every day."

Danny shook her head vigorously. "No, I want to live in the town where I work. I don't want to be just a figurehead at the company; I want to be a part of the community. I think that's very important."

"That's about as futile has having your cake and eating it too." They stopped walking and stood facing one another.

"Perhaps it is," Danny mused, "but I'm determined to try." Her eyes gleamed in defiance.

Logan shrugged. "No one's to say what you can or can't do. I'm just saying that your becoming a part of the Blaketon community may be an impossible dream."

"No," she whispered, "it's not an impossible dream. I

know it won't come true today or tomorrow, but it will come true. I'm going to make it come true."

"Okay." He had heard flinty resolve in her declaration. Before she knew what he was doing, he took her hands in his and patted them supportively. Who was he to argue with her? "How about our going for a ride to blow the cobwebs out and to finish our discussion?"

Danny shook her head. "Not tonight. I'm tired. I've had a busy day, and I have to be up early in the morning." Wanting to put some distance between her and Logan, she stepped away, but Logan increased his stride and walked alongside her.

"Before I leave tonight, I'd like to talk about the campaign. Nothing definitive. But at least we'll each know where the other is coming from, and we can come up with some basic ideas." His hand closed over her elbow and his fingers held her soft flesh firmly as he guided her to a secluded corner of the lobby that overlooked the Cape Fear River. He gave her no opportunity to deny his suggestion. After they sat down, she on the sofa, he on the chair opposite her, he asked, "Anything else you need to tell me about Blaketon Pharmaceuticals. Any more obstacles we need to hurdle in order to get this company on its feet?" He wanted to get business out of the way so he could discover more about Danella Jones the woman.

Danny shrugged, sinking into the softness of the seat, letting the warmth and the music that drifted from the lounge take effect, relaxing her a little bit. "I don't know that this will affect your work," she told him, "but it'll definitely affect mine, and I think I'd better tell you about it." As much as she distrusted him personally, she knew enough of his reputation to trust his professional judgment completely. She took a deep breath and gazed out the window. "Because Lethia wasn't hired as manager and because I've been transferred to that position, I'm losing several of my key personnel."

She didn't take her eyes off the river, which reflected the bright lights of the waterfront buildings, but Logan could hear the heaviness in her voice. "One of my first official duties will be to sign their transfers." She sighed. "It would be so much better if I could just keep them; they're an established part of the community. The community knows and accepts them, and they know the community. More than that, they know their jobs."

"It seems to me that that's something someone in your position should have to expect. It's something you're going to have to put up with, Danny girl."

Danny wanted to scream at him; she wanted to demand that he stop using her nickname, but she didn't want to let him know that he was affecting her at all. So she turned her face to his, her acceptance obvious in her expression. "If Lethia would speak to these people and reassure them, they would hold off on their transfers. They would give me a chance. But she won't. She's not giving me any support at all."

"Of course not. She must feel awful that an outsider, a twenty-nine-year-old woman at that, has been brought in as the head of the company that her grandfather began at the turn of the century. She's been knocked down from her pedestal in the community and she's running scared. She's probably wondering what's going to happen to her social prestige."

"I know," Danella said. "I've tried to put myself in her shoes, but . . ." She shook her head in exasperation.

"When are you officially taking over?"

"Next week."

"The first of November. We'll be working through Thanksgiving and Christmas?"

"Yes, we will. Do you mind?" She was so concerned about the plant and her employees, Danny hadn't given a thought to the holidays.

He shrugged. "I don't have anything better planned

for Thanksgiving and Christmas than the promotion of Blaketon Pharmaceuticals."

His off-handed answer whetted Danny's curiosity. "What about your family? Maybe they have something planned that would include you."

"Just the usual kind of family get together, but I imagine if work dictates, you can spare me one of the special days, can't you?"

"No, I can't," was the quick response. "I already have plans that don't include you." Then she asked, "But if I were to spare you a day, which one would you want? Thanksgiving or Christmas?"

"I'll spend Thanksgiving with the family and Christmas with you."

"Shouldn't that be the other way around?"

"Depends on the person," he countered, tilting his head back.

Danny didn't like the intimacy that this man could generate; she didn't like the sensuality that seemed to exude from him without the slightest exertion on his part. He was too dangerous for her to be around. Already she found herself liking him. He was that persuasive and she was that gullible. Irritated with herself, she turned and observed the people who were milling around the lobby. She didn't plan on being another Jackie Wesson.

Turning to him again, she said, "If this is all, I think I'll turn in." She smiled mechanically, the gesture involving only her lips. "I'm rather tired."

Logan nodded, wondering why she was so averse to being with him. He'd spent the evening with her, yet he felt she had never really been with him. Consciously she responded to his conversation but subconsciously she was somewhere else. Grasping at any reason to keep her with him a little longer, he said, "You know, I feel like I ought to know you." He shook his head. "But

I just can't place you. Which branch have you been working at?"

"Atlanta, mostly, but I've worked at branch offices in Chicago, Mississippi, and Florida."

"Odd that I've never seen you," he mused. "Atlanta, you say. . . ." He pursed his lips, thinking, finally saying, "Maybe I saw you there. Let's see three or four . . ." He lapsed into silence as he began to calculate the time. "No," he suddenly exclaimed, laughing as he corrected himself. "Goes to show you how fast time flies. It's been more like four, nearly five years since I was in Atlanta, working for Warrington."

"I know."

"You know." His brow furrowed. "But we didn't meet."

"No, we didn't meet directly." So soft was her answer that Logan never heard the suppressed bitterness. "In fact, I never even saw you. Just heard about you."

She had Logan's full attention. "From your statement and from your tone, I have the distinct feeling that you don't like me based on what you heard."

"You went with my friend, Jackie Wesson," Danella said, intentionally dropping the name. Then she looked at him, wanting to see his reaction, waiting for his response. When he evinced no emotion at all, she was disappointed.

"More like we worked together," Logan corrected. "We were working on Warrington's acquisition of Sykes and Son." As the details cleared up he nodded his head, smiling apologetically. "It's been so long that I'd almost forgotten."

How could you forget? Danella silently screamed. *You had an affair with her!*

"How's she doing now?" he asked, and Danella could tell by his voice that he really didn't care. It was just a polite inquiry.

Danella stared unbelievingly at him. "She's dead,

Logan. She committed suicide a few months after you left." The dull words, like the steady, heavy blows of a hammer, resounded through the lobby. "She died with your name on her lips."

Logan's face was a mask of shocked surprise. "My name—" Why would Jackie have called his name in death? Eventually, however, he murmured, "I'm sorry. I didn't know."

Danella's anger left her speechless. What kind of game was Logan Spencer playing? "The hospital tried to reach you. . . ." Saying no more, she shrugged, again taking refuge in watching the lights as they played on the water of the river.

"I must have been out of the country at the time," he explained. "As soon as I finished the assignment for Horace, I flew to Europe." Softly he pleaded, "I never received a message, Danny. I don't know why she would have wanted to see me, but I would have come."

Logan's confession touched Danella, but she refused to let herself believe him. She remembered what he had done to Jackie. She would never forget. She wouldn't let herself forget!

"Logan"—she hardly spoke the word, but the expression on her face compelled him to lean forward—"you and I are going to have to work together. But understand this: All we're going to do is work together." Her eyes were pewter gray, hard and cold.

The blue eyes sadly raked over her face. "Is Jackie the reason why you dislike me, Danella?" The question was gentle and in direct contrast to the chiseled hardness of his face, in direct contrast to all that she'd heard about him. "Is she the reason why you're so antagonistic?"

Danny stared at him for several seconds before she said, "You knew that Jackie was in love with you!"

Logan didn't respond immediately to her accusation. He was loath to discuss that portion of his private life with Danella. He had never been one to subscribe to the kiss-and-tell philosophy. But at the same time he knew his answer was important to her. "I knew that she would like for it to be more than what it was."

"When I returned from Chicago," Danella mused, "I found her a changed woman. All she could talk about was you." She paused, swallowed the tears that knotted her throat, and continued, "I was with her the Friday evening before she . . . before she died."

Danella's gaze was locked to Logan's face, and she saw all the emotions that flickered across it. Although his face mirrored his shock and his sadness, she could tell that it wasn't grief for Jackie. Danella instantly knew it was for her. He was thinking about the hurt she had suffered. He was concerned about her grief over the suicide of her friend. Danny couldn't understand Logan. How could he be so unconcerned about Jackie's death and at the same time be so concerned about Danella's reaction to it? But, she decided, shrugging her puzzlement and questions aside, if he wanted to play the innocent, let him. As long as he and she were only business associates, she couldn't care less about his personal life.

"And you blame me for her death?"

Danella lifted her hand to her face and pressed her fingers to her lips. When she spoke, her words were muffled. "Your rejection was the one rejection she couldn't bear."

"Danny . . ." With fluid grace he moved from the chair to the sofa and placed one hand comfortingly on her thigh. "I didn't lead your friend on. We worked together on a project, and we had several business dates, but it was never more than that. I didn't lead her on." His other hand gently held her chin and guided her face to his. "I promise you." The deep, mellow timbre of his voice dropped to a husky whisper. "Please believe me."

Danella gazed at him for an eternity before evad-

31

ing the branding touch of his hand, breaking the hypnotic gaze that begged for her trust. She began to smooth imaginary wrinkles from her jacket. "It doesn't really matter whether I believe you or not, Logan. Personal likes and dislikes won't affect our working together." She maneuvered herself forward, easing out of the softness of the cushions, farther away from the warmth and strength of Logan's body. "I think I'll call it a night," she sighed more than spoke. "I'm really quite tired."

"Don't go!" Logan's low voice was gentle. When she lifted her face to him in question, he said, "Not yet." He knew he couldn't let her return to her room; she was still too upset. "Since we've got to work together, let's get acquainted."

Although it shouldn't have, Logan's quiet request surprised Danny, and she just looked at him. She knew she should leave, but at the same time she didn't want to. She didn't want to return to the small, lonely hotel room.

Perceiving her acquiescence, Logan softly asked, "Are you from Atlanta or did your job take you there?"

"I was born and raised in Augusta, but I attended college in Atlanta. I've been there ever since."

"So this is your first time away from your stomping ground?" He was looking desperately for a hole in the wall of reserve of bitterness and hatred behind which Danny hid.

"Yes." She added no more. Whatever he wanted to know he would have to ask to find out; she was volunteering nothing.

Lapsing into another period of silence, they both stared out the window, his gaze running along the horizontal line of water. "Are you afraid of us liking each other?"

"Absolutely not. I just don't see the necessity of our liking one another." Danny stood and walked out onto

32

the balcony. Throwing her head back, she lifted her face to the wind. Its touch stung her cheeks, just as Logan's presence and words were whipping against her reserves, battering them down. "If you want me to say I like you," she announced when he stood next to her, "then I'll say it, but it's just words. Don't look for more."

"I think before it's over, Danella Jones, you're the one who will be looking for more. And when you do, you'll find me ready and willing to be your friend." Again his gentleness touched her, and again it disconcerted her because it was so contrary to the portrait of Logan Spencer that Jackie had painted. Adroitly he changed the subject, surprising Danny with his sudden move. "Is there a special someone in your life?"

"Yes," Danella said emphatically, hoping that this revelation would end their conversation.

"Tell me about him."

Grudgingly, Danny began to talk. It was better, she decided, if all this was out in the open. Then there could be no misunderstandings. "His name's Brock Singleton. He works with Bloomington Aircraft in Atlanta."

"How'd he take the transfer?"

"Both of us are career-oriented," Danny explained quite matter-of-factly. "He was happy for me. Naturally he didn't want me to leave, but he knew how important this job was to me."

Logan laughed disdainfully. "If he cared for you, he wouldn't have let you leave. If it had been me, I would have done anything to get you to stay."

"That's the difference between you and Brock."

"Maybe that's the difference between love and like," Logan pointed out softly. "That's why you feel safe with liking someone. Like makes no demands. You're afraid of something deeper. You're afraid that you'll meet a

33

man who will have a right to make demands in your life."

"No," she refuted, not allowing him to get her all riled up. "I'm not afraid of something deeper, but neither am I worried that I won't find something deeper. I don't have any hang-ups about it one way or the other."

"Does your being career-oriented preclude the possibility of marriage?"

"You're getting rather personal, Logan. My life is no concern of yours. I'm not interested in marriage, and I have no interest in discussing it further with you."

"But in any acquaintance between an eligible male and female, it's a distinct possibility," he continued as if baiting her. "One that must be thought about. And if I'm annoying you, that's not so bad. I'm glad to know that I'm affecting you." He smiled, sliding closer to her. "At least you're not indifferent."

No, Danny thought, *I'm not indifferent. I wish I were, but I'm not*. She pulled a hand out of her pocket to brush the hair out of her eyes and her mouth. She could understand a woman's falling in love with Logan Spencer. He had a way about him.

"Tell me something about your family," she said, feeling she had to change the course of the conversation.

"My father and mother own a farm not far from Charlotte," he said easily, leaning against the banister. "I'm the oldest, with a younger sister who's married to a doctor. They live in Charlotte and have a nine-year-old son, Ryan Thomas, called Tommy by family and friends." Without missing a breath, he asked, "How about you?"

He hadn't told her very much about himself, so she answered his question with the same skimpy facts that he'd given her. "My parents live in Augusta, where Dad is a contractor with his own company. I'm the oldest. Three sisters and a baby brother."

Then, as Logan began to talk again, happily describing his family, Danella studied his profile, again noticing the slightly flattened nose. Much later, after he had lapsed into a comfortable silence, she said, "From the looks of you, you haven't always been the suave sophisticate, Logan Spencer."

"Oh?" he lazily droned, slowly turning his head in her direction.

"I'd say from the shape of your nose that you've played some rough sports in your life."

Logan reached up and rubbed his fingers across his nose. "Yeah, I played football. All the way through high school and college. Athletic scholarships. Actually I even wanted to go pro, but it turned out that I didn't have either the ability or the dedication." He rubbed his nose again and grinned at her, friendly lines curving around the corners of his mouth, laugh lines fanning at the edges of his eyes. Taking advantage of her momentary warming, Logan suggested, "Let's go inside and get a drink, and if you're in the mood, we can dance to the music of the band. For a local group, they're one of the best."

Still not ready to return to her room but also not ready to spend time in the intimacy of the lounge with Logan, Danny hesitated. A drink sounded good. She was chilled to the bone. The dancing? She wasn't so sure about that. Yet, she couldn't help feeling a certain curiosity. What would it be like to be held in his arms? What would it feel like to move to the beat of the music in his embrace?

She pushed the chaotic and rebellious thoughts aside, angry with herself because she could be physically attracted to a man she despised. Struggling for a lightness that she didn't feel, she said, "Thanks but no, thanks." She pushed away from the banister. "I'm ready to call it a night."

"Just one drink, Danny," Logan said in a low voice that was as soft as velvet.

Danny, imprisoned by his compelling gaze, almost wanted to say yes. And if it had been any other man, she would have. But not Logan Spencer. She shook her head as, unbidden, the image of Jackie Wesson insinuated itself between the two of them. She saw the shoulder-length black hair that framed the slender, oval face. She saw the blue eyes that were dull with hopelessness; she heard the sobs of anguish and despair. She tried to push Jackie aside, wishing the haunting memories would go away, hating this man for having resurrected them.

Danella's expression hardened. For several moments she and Logan stared at each other. Finally she folded her arms across her breasts and shivered with anxiety and apprehension. But when she spoke, her tones were smooth, giving no evidence of her inner turmoil.

"I'd like for us to get to work on the publicity as soon as possible. When do you think you could show me a tentative schedule of your campaign?"

"Dinner tomorrow evening?" Logan suggested, a hopeful smile curving his lips.

Again Danella shook her head. "I think there are enough hours in the working day for meetings." She moved across the balcony, reentering the lobby of the hotel. Her hand closed over the doorknob, but before she opened the door, she added for good measure, "I know I don't want you intruding into my personal life after hours."

As Danella lay in her bed later, she knew the folly of her words. Since she had returned to her room, she hadn't been able to get Logan Spencer out of her mind. Against her will and her better judgment, he had intruded into her thoughts. And if she wasn't careful, she knew he would invade her life.

CHAPTER TWO

The sound of someone rapping on the door interrupted Danella, and she looked up from the stat sheets she had been slaving over since lunch. When she saw Lethia Blake standing in the doorway, she smiled, her eyes admiringly taking in the tall, shapely woman in the black Halston dress. Danella could never get over how beautiful Lethia was. Although she was over forty, her dark brown hair with its silver streak, her amber eyes, and her flawless complexion made her both a stunning and aristocratic-looking woman.

"Good afternoon, Lethia. What can I do for you?"

Danella squared her shoulders, her left hand automatically straightening the ruffle at her neck. She looked the picture of poise, her head high, her carriage speaking self-confidence.

"I hope I'm not interrupting anything," Lethia began in her patrician accent. She walked into the office and sat in one of the chairs in front of Danella's desk. She lifted a hand to her elegantly coiffed hair, lightly touching the deep waves, which swept into a French twist.

Then her hand dropped, her fingers caressing the long double strand of pearls around her neck.

Danny flicked her wrist and looked at her watch. "Just working on the day-care–center project. Nothing that can't wait," she replied, leaning back, dropping her pen on the desk, and waiting for Lethia to speak.

"I wanted to talk with you, but you've been so busy this morning that I haven't had a chance." Lethia's amber eyes were gently accusing. "I thought perhaps you were avoiding me because of yesterday."

"No," Danny stated, remembering Lethia's refusal to talk with Grodon Bowen and Lawrence Curtis, the two supervisors who wanted immediate transfers. "I've just been so busy. I had a long meeting with Curtis and Bowen that lasted all morning, and I had a report for Mr. Warrington that had to get out today."

Lethia nodded her acknowledgment. "I've been thinking about the conversation that we had yesterday afternoon, and I hope I didn't anger you." She smiled and lowered her voice to a placating softness. "I didn't mean to."

"No . . . you just disappointed me."

Lethia looked wounded. "And I think perhaps you've deliberately misunderstood my motives, Danella."

Danny shrugged. "Perhaps, but it still amounts to your not giving me your support when I need it the most." Danny sighed, wondering if she could ever win against this woman. Lethia was not just a martyr to the people of the firm and the community; she was practically a venerated saint. In fact, she was the patron saint of Blaketon. "Those transfers are taking two men out of our office and plant whom we desperately need right now—two men whose expertise we can hardly afford to lose."

Lethia smiled patronizingly and lifted a hand, caressing her cheek with her fingertips. "I'm sorry that you

38

can't understand my position, Danella, but I can't and I won't ask these men to stay. You've studied the financial records, and you, better than anyone, should know that Blake Company failed because production and sales had dropped so drastically." Her voice rose slightly and her manner became vaguely defiant. "And as I pointed out yesterday, the production failure was rooted in conflict between Curtis and Bowen and management." Her voice grew more assertive as she accused. "The same key personnel whom you want to keep, Danella, are the reasons why Blake Company declared bankruptcy." Emotion had knotted in Lethia's throat; her voice was high with tension; and her hands were clenched into tight fists. "I believe you're dooming Blaketon Pharmaceuticals from its inception if you insist on keeping Bowen and Curtis."

"Lethia, believe me, I understand what you're saying; I can understand your feelings. But you've also got to admit that a great deal of the responsibility for those past conflicts must also be shouldered by management and its failure to get along with the workers, to listen to them, to talk with them, and to let them have input in the company. I'm introducing a new concept in management, and I think I can work with these people, so I'm going to give them a second chance. Not only that, but I plan to change company policy. I'm going to listen to the workers and communicate with them, and any attempt on anyone's part, no matter whose, to hinder me will be met with strictest disciplinary action." Danella's voice turned to a pleading softness. "And you can help me, if you will, Lethia."

Lethia laughed quietly. "I think, Danella, that you equate help with granting all your desires. And that shall never be. I'm for Blaketon Pharmaceuticals, not Danella Jones. I will not offer my support on any issue with which I'm in such complete disagreement."

39

Danella tensed. "May I remind you that at this time Blaketon Pharmaceuticals's survival depends largely on Danella Jones and her ability to salvage that which you and your family were unable to save. I understand that you are used to being in control here, but at the moment there's room for only one person at the helm of Blaketon Pharmaceuticals. That person, Lethia, like it or not, is me. If you choose to remain with the company, please remember that at all times." Danella straightened her shoulders and looked squarely at the older woman.

Lethia stood, walked to the door, and opened it before she turned to look at Danella. A strange smile played on her lips. "I'll give this some thought, Danella, but it'll do you good to remember who *I* am and the role *I* play in this community."

"The main reason why you're still a part of this company is out of respect to your family's position in the community," Danella shot back. "But respect, Lethia, can be stretched only so far without breaking. The success of this company takes precedence over any individual's respect. No one will be exempt from disciplinary actions if he or she in any way hinders me."

Lethia sighed. "In the very near future, Danella Jones," she said softly, "I think you'll find out just how important a commodity I am to Blaketon Pharmaceuticals. I daresay that you'll eventually come around to my way of thinking."

With those words she walked out of the office, leaving Danella to ponder the truth of her pronouncement. Danella shook her head and lifted her hands to her temples. She felt a headache coming, and she knew why: She was still keyed up from her meeting with Bowen and Curtis that morning; she was concerned about the report that she had sent the home office; and she was worried about the day-care center that Lethia and her following were opposing.

40

But Danella didn't give in to the dull throbbing in her temples; rather, she picked up a file of papers that she needed typed and carried them into the outer office. Handing them to her secretary, Ona Winfield, she smiled and asked, "Will you add these to the minutes you took this morning, Ona? Since I'll need them in communiqué form by Monday, I'd like for you to type them this afternoon. That way I can make any necessary corrections, and we'll have them ready to be sent out to all the unit managers by Wednesday."

Ona lifted her round face to Danella, took the papers, and quickly glanced through them. Then she looked at the clock on the wall. Three-thirty! She sighed. Oh, well, it wouldn't take her too long to type them, and she could get back to the files that had to be completed before she went home. She pulled the pencil from behind her ear and patted her small, chubby hand against the short white curls that framed her face.

As she corrected a misspelled word she said, "I'll have this to you in about twenty minutes, Ms. Jones, and we'll be ready to make the corrections Monday morning." She reached for her glasses, which lay on the desk, and turned to her word processor.

Danella walked into her office, sighing deeply and feeling suddenly deflated. She stood at the window and stared at the beautifully landscaped lawn that surrounded Blaketon Pharmaceuticals. The November day was dismal and gloomy. Large gray clouds stretched darkly across the sky, and rain threatened to fall at any moment. Periodically flashes of lightning appeared in the blackness, followed by an ominous boom of thunder.

She felt like the weather looked, Danny thought glumly, pushing a hand through her hair. She had known that her takeover of Blaketon Pharmaceuticals would be difficult, but she hadn't imagined it being like this. She felt like an island unto herself. She had no one

41

to confide in—no one to give her advice. She could call her father, but she didn't want to bother him. He had enough worries of his own. And she couldn't call Horace Warrington; she wanted to handle this by herself.

Then the pensive silence was broken by the shrill ring of the telephone. Picking up the receiver, she said, "Danella Jones."

"A long-distance phone call from Brock Singleton," Ona's brisk voice came through the line. "Want to take it?"

"Brock," Danella repeated, surprise and happiness lifting her voice. She couldn't imagine why he was calling. He should be on his way to Blaketon at that moment. "Yes! Yes, I'll take it."

"I kinda figured you would. He sounds sexy." Ona chuckled softly, saying as she rang off, "Line three."

Danny's fingers raced over the buttons, and she said breathlessly, "Brock! Is that really you?"

"Yes, Danella, it's me." A deep, resonant voice full of amusement flowed through the line.

"Oh, Brock," Danny cried, sinking into the cushioned chair behind her desk. What a godsend! His voice had never sounded lovelier, nor had she ever wanted to hear it as badly. "I'm so glad you called." At least, this was a bright spot in her otherwise dreary day. "What time are you going to get here?"

"Oh, Lord, Danny girl," Brock said apologetically. "That's what I'm calling about. I'm going to have to cancel out this weekend."

"No, Brock!" Danella couldn't help the small cry of disappointment. She couldn't stand many more letdowns in one day.

"I'm sorry, Danny, but there's an aeronautics seminar at Randolph Air Force base in San Antonio, and Dwight insists that I attend it." The timbre of his voice lowered. "I've got to go, sweetheart. I'm scheduled to fly out in a couple of hours."

"I know." She paused, adding tentatively, "I wish you could come, though. I need to see you."

Danella wanted to tell him exactly how she felt. She needed him this weekend; she wanted his company. But she didn't say anything; there was nothing he could do about it. She understood his having to attend the seminar, but she wanted him to insist that she come to him. However, she knew he wouldn't. They had agreed from the outset of their relationship never to intrude on each other's career.

"I'm going to miss you, Danny," he cooed. "Spending all my weekend at a seminar in San Antonio with Amy Denvers isn't exactly what I call a special time."

"Amy Denvers?" Danella asked quietly, having no difficulty conjuring up the image of the pretty redhead she had met at one of Brock's office parties.

"Yeah," he drawled. "You know the one who works . . ."

As he continued to talk Danella listened, not really interested in Amy Denvers but wondering just how interested Brock was in her.

"I . . ." She moistened her dry lips with her tongue. "I guess I could meet you in San Antonio, Brock."

"I'd love that," he immediately assented, his voice excited and animated. Then he slowly sighed. "Oh, honey, that wouldn't be fair to you. We wouldn't be able to see each other. I'm going to have to stay in base housing, and I'd be in the seminar most of the time." The disappointment was evident in his voice. "Let's make it another weekend, sweetheart—one when we can be together without other things on our mind, without our jobs interfering."

Reluctantly, Danny agreed, seeing the logic of his argument. Then they talked without really saying anything important. Finally, just before Brock hung up, he said, "If we don't get together before then, I'll see you Thanksgiving. Probably spend the day with you."

43

Danella swiveled around in her chair and gazed out the large window, her mind on company problems, and her heart already exhausted. "I doubt it, Brock. I'll probably be spending Thanksgiving here."

"Oh?"

Danella could understand his dismay, but, like him, she had a job to do. "I'll only have the day, so I won't be able to come home."

"I—I was counting on it," Brock said, sounding hurt. "We've always spent Thanksgiving together at your parents' place."

"I know, but not this Thanksgiving."

After Danella explained why she couldn't take more time off, they hung up. She continued to sit in her chair, staring out the window, watching the wind as it chased the black clouds around the sky, pushing them closer and closer to the ground, creating a cloak of darkness. She might just fly to Augusta this weekend, she thought, a lone tear making its way down her cheek. It would do her good to see her family. It would certainly cheer her up. Even if their schedules were hectic, they would readjust them so they could spend their time with her.

Then the telephone rang a second time and she answered it, her voice dull. "Danella Jones." She lifted her hand and swiped at her wet cheek.

"Logan Spencer is here."

"Logan." She hadn't expected him until the following Monday. "Ona, just wait a minute or two, then send him in," she said.

Doing her best to regain her aplomb, Danny dropped the phone onto the cradle and waited for the door to open. When Logan walked into the room, her eyes appreciatively ran over his massive frame, taking in the charcoal gray slacks, the long-sleeved blue sweater, and the white shirt, the collar barely peeking above the rounded neckline of the sweater. His blue eyes were accented by the color of the sweater.

The easy grin that Danella remembered from the other night spread across his face. "Well, Ms. Danella Jones, you're a sight for sore eyes." Logan quickly assessed the trim figure colorfully garbed in the red suit. The grin turned to a smile, and a soft chuckle rumbled from his thick chest. "In fact, you're a sight for any eyes."

Danella propped her elbows on the armrests of her chair, and she wove her fingers together. Before she could help herself or stop the reflexive action, a smile curved her lips. "Believe it or not, Logan Spencer, I am glad to see you too."

As Logan sat in the large chair in front of Danella's desk he raised an eyebrow in surprise. "Dare I believe my ears?

Danella actually laughed with him. "You may. I'm interested in seeing what you have planned for our publicity."

"Work," he scoffed. "That's the only reason you're glad to see me? You haven't been curious about me at all? You haven't wondered what it would be like to go out with me?"

"I thought I made it quite plain that our relationship began and ended with business."

Her words didn't daunt him at all. He just shrugged his shoulders, accepting the challenge. "Danny girl, if I keep trying long enough, you'll eventually agree to go out with me."

That was exactly what she would avoid at all costs, Danella thought, looking across the desk at him. She chuckled. "I advise you to give up now, Logan. You're just wasting your time."

"Thank you for the concern," he conceded with a twinkle, "but I never just give up. You'll learn as you get to know me better that I don't concede defeat easily. And I never waste my time; I specialize in wooing and winning beautiful women."

Upon uttering the teasing words, Logan saw a shadow cross Danella's eyes, and he knew instantly that she was remembering Jackie. Quickly, adroitly, he led the subject away from that painful topic. They exchanged more remarks as he tried to keep their conversation light. Finally, however, Danella changed the subject, moving to the matter of work.

"I assume your coming today rather than Monday is because you have good news."

"I think so," he replied. "I've mapped out our preliminary campaign, but I need to go over it with you to confirm dates and all."

"I've also been doing some thinking and some figuring during the past week, and I've come up with some ideas I wanted to share with you. I'd like your opinion on them before I put them into operation."

Logan eased back in the chair, lifting one leg and folding it so that the ankle rested on the other leg. He recognized that tone of voice. He'd heard clients use it before. And he knew it could mean only one thing: It didn't mean they wanted his opinion on the subject; it meant they wanted his sanction. He could tell that Danella already had her ideas planned and packaged. She was ready to hand it to him now. She was ready for him to execute her little maneuvers.

"I'm willing to listen," he told her amiably and carefully, "but I'll make no promises—"

A soft series of raps on the door interrupted his sentence, and he looked over his shoulder as Danella said, "Come in."

For the second time that afternoon, Lethia entered Danella's office, her perfume announcing her arrival almost before she could be seen. "Sorry I'm late," she apologized breathlessly to Logan, her amber eyes quickly scanning Danella's surprised countenance before returning her gaze to Logan's face.

Danella couldn't hide her incredulity. What was Lethia doing there? she wondered, and why was she apologizing to Logan for being late? As if he could read minds, Logan looked at Danella.

"Hope you don't mind. I stopped by Ms. Blake's office on the way to yours and asked her to meet with us."

Danella shook her head. "No, of course I don't mind. As the assistant manager, I expect her to be an active part of our publicity campaign."

"Good," Logan said, standing and walking to the round table in the corner of her office. He glanced at Lethia, who had followed him to the table, and smiled. "And with your permission we're going to capitalize on her being a Blake. She's going to be the media spokesperson for Blaketon Pharmaceuticals."

It was a full minute before Danella could break out of the shock that had paralyzed her. Why hadn't she been informed that Lethia was to be the spokesperson for Blaketon Pharmaceuticals? Why had Logan so callously broken the news to her like that?

Logan, unaware of Danella's shock, turned toward her. "If you'll join us, I'll show you what I've been doing these past two weeks and what I've got planned." He laid his briefcase on the table and opened it, spreading his material across the top as Danella slowly walked toward him. After she was seated beside Lethia, he began to outline his campaign. "We'll want to take shots of the grounds, the plant, and the workers themselves. These are sketches of the first series." He tapped the drawings with his index finger as he talked. "I'd like for all of our commercials to be done with Blaketon employees."

Leaning over the table, looking at the layouts, Lethia nodded and enthusiastically murmured her agreement.

Danny sat back, saying nothing, just listening and watching. She had managed to keep her anger under control all day, but right now she felt as if she could barely restrain her fury. She realized what a volcano must be like just before it erupted, belching its venomous gas and fiery liquid on unsuspecting victims.

"Playing a hunch," Logan confessed huskily, "Lethia called me when she uncovered a family history on the Blakes and the company. She gave me some ideas that I'd like to share with you."

Lethia flashed Danella a bright smile and handed Logan the file. "That's why I was late. Ethel and I were doing some last-minute editing and revising." She smiled. "This is just a rough draft, Logan, but it'll give you some idea of what I'm doing."

Logan grinned in appreciation as he leafed through the pages. "This is fantastic, Lethia. Just what I need."

Danella couldn't stop the anger that shot through her body. She couldn't believe that Logan had allowed Lethia to do this to her. "Why am I the last to be told?" she asked quietly.

Logan looked at her blankly for a second, then shook his head. "I'm sorry, Danella. I just never thought—"

Lethia said, "The idea just came to me on the spur of the moment, Danella, and I immediately thought about Logan." She smiled apologetically. "I certainly didn't mean to go over your head."

Not fully understanding the tension that crackled between the two women, Logan chuckled. "Hardly. And I needed to think about it first so I could have some idea what we were going to do with it." He grinned and said "Sorry," dismissing Danella's grievance. "We're going to start out on *Arlene Wideman's Morning Show*, Lethia. Here are the dates. Which one would be best for you?"

Lethia laughed, her excitement causing her eyes to

dance. "Either one will be fine with me." She beamed. "You choose, Logan." She looked from Danella to Logan, grinning. "I can't imagine myself on TV. Do you think I can do it?"

"Sure you can. You'll be fantastic," Logan told her, delighted with her response, and over several cups of coffee they discussed publicity, setting up and confirming media interviews and press releases in all the surrounding towns. After he had recorded all the dates in his log, Logan gathered his materials and slid them into his briefcase.

"Logan," Danella said, standing, walking to her desk and picking up a file, "I'd like for my projected day-care center to be a part of the publicity." She returned to the table and handed the manila folder to him. "I think it would be a terrific attention-getter."

"In more than one way," Lethia retorted. "Although it's a wonderful concept, it's more idealistic than pragmatic at the moment. You're moving much too fast for Blaketon."

Ignoring Lethia's barbed comments, Danny quickly outlined for Logan her proposed company-operated day-care center, carefully pointing out the advantages. By the time she had concluded her presentation, Logan was leisurely slouching on the sofa.

"I have to agree with Lethia," he said, carelessly raking his hand through his hair. "If you start making changes this quick, you might scare some people." He smiled, trying to soften the blow of his refusal when he saw disappointment in Danny's eyes. "Don't take offense at what I'm about to say, Danella, but you're an outsider and you don't understand the mentality of these people."

Seething but curbing her anger, Danella said, "Perhaps you would explain, then, Mr. Spencer, what the mentality of these people is. Perhaps with your help I can become an insider."

"This is a small rural community, Danella, and the majority of the people feel that a woman should remain at home, taking care of her children. She should let her husband earn the living. If we advertise this company-operated day-care center, the public might feel that we were openly and blatantly enticing women away from their homes and their children."

"That's antiquated thinking," Danella stated, fighting to keep the disappointment at bay.

"Nonetheless, Danella," Logan responded, "that's the way it is. This is an insular southern community where people have different values from those to which you're accustomed." Then he added with finality, giving her idea a death blow, "Furthermore, we're not going to advertise this at the beginning." He opened his organizer and jotted some notes. "We'll save this for later in the campaign, when we see how well it's functioning—when it's an accomplished and successful fact."

Trying to accept her defeat graciously, Danny shuffled her papers in her file, snapped the folder closed, and returned to her desk. Just as she dropped the file in the organizer Lethia spoke.

"Logan, have you thought about publicizing the Blake Christmas tradition?" A strange smile played on her lips.

Logan picked up his empty cup and walked to the bar, pouring himself more coffee. "The grist mill and the famed forest." He nodded his head. "That's a good idea, Lethia."

Danny almost gasped with hurt and irritation. She didn't know whom she resented more, Logan or Lethia.

Logan glanced at Danny and, thinking she didn't know what Lethia was talking about, explained. "To the people of Blaketon the grist mill and the surrounding forest is the established institution as well as a tradition. Both of these distinguish them from all other communities in the area."

"Christmas Tree Forest," Lethia recounted dreamily, "begun in the early 1900's by my great-grandfather, Leonard Morely Blake, and continued through the years by each successive Blake. However, in recent years it has dwindled to almost nothing." She walked to the bookcases on the wall opposite Danella's desk and pulled out several photograph albums. "Here are the photographs." She sat down next to Logan, turning the pages and describing the different ideas as they looked at the pictures.

"This year," Logan said, "Blaketon Pharmaceuticals will provide a Christmas Tree Forest that will outdo all others." Sensing that Danella felt left out, he looked at her. "Here's your chance to prove your mettle to these people."

"Me?" Danny cried indignantly. He hadn't wanted her for the public appearances; he hadn't wanted her to be the spokesperson; but he wanted her to be the behind-the-scenes supervisor for this community Christmas project. He was letting Lethia be in the limelight while Danella remained in the background.

"You," Logan answered, quickly flipping through his organizer and writing notes. "This will catch the public's eye, and at what better time than Christmas?" He looked up and grinned at her. "By the time we're done, the community will love you as much as they love Lethia."

Danella shook her head. "I don't think so, Logan. Local folklore isn't my speciality. I think Lethia is the better person for this job. She's the Cinderella around here; I'm just the wicked stepsister."

Danny's bitter words tickled Lethia, and the latter chuckled. "I should like very much to organize Christmas Tree Forest, Danella, but Logan is right: You're the manager of Blaketon Pharmaceuticals, and as such you're the community leader. Besides, I'm going to be tied up with all other aspects of Logan's campaign." Her golden eyes sparkled with challenge. "If you're sincere about your priority being Blaketon Pharmaceuticals and Blaketon, then you should tackle this."

"I'll think about it," Danella murmured.

Logan lifted his arm and looked at his wristwatch. "Good gracious!" he exclaimed. "I didn't realize it was this late. I've got to go." He smiled at Lethia. "Ready?"

Nodding, Lethia said, "Let me clean off my desk and lock up my office."

"Logan," Danella barked, not understanding the irritation she felt over Logan's familiarity with Lethia, "may I see you alone before you leave?"

Logan looked at Lethia, who said, "I'll meet you in the parking lot."

After the door closed behind Lethia, Danny, still stinging because Logan hadn't consulted her before contacting Lethia, asked, "Do you realize how you made me look in front of her?"

Logan lifted his thick sandy brows questioningly and shook his head.

"Here I am, fighting to win the support of these people, trying to salvage this company. It isn't enough that the people ignore me, going directly to Lethia, but then the public relations adviser does the same thing."

Understanding her argument, Logan raised a hand and ran it through his hair. "I'm sorry, Danella. I didn't mean to put you in a bad light. But Lethia didn't mean anything by coming directly to me about the Blake history. And I promise I won't do anything that would hurt or upset you or your efforts to save the company." His voice lowered to a tender murmur. "Besides, her calling me had nothing to do with you."

"But it had everything to do with me," she argued. "Mr. Warrington made me the division manager, and everything that goes with Blaketon Pharmaceuticals is my concern—publicity and all!"

"You're the manager," Logan stoutly contested, firmly delineating the difference in their jobs, "I'm in charge of public relations. And that's the way we're going to run this show. You handle your area; I'll take care of mine. I don't have time to pamper your ego by calling every time I want to make a move."

"Pamper my ego," Danny exclaimed on a deadly whisper. "It's got nothing to do with my ego. This happens to be my job, Logan Spencer. And for your information, my area is the entire cake, remember? So you will call me and inform me of every move that you're making." Her voice rose even higher. "You will let me know every move that you *intend* to make."

"If I remember correctly, Ms. Danella Jones, you didn't hire me for this job. Horace J. Warrington did, and I'll answer to him and not to you."

"We'll just see about that," Danella snapped. "First thing Monday morning, I'll call Mr. Warrington and have him tell me that out of his own mouth. Until such time as he tells me that, Mr. Spencer, *you will account to me.*"

Suddenly, Logan began to chuckle, the soft sound soon turning into a deep, mellow rumble. "You know, Danella Jones, I think you're finally showing some signs of being human. I think you're jealous."

"Not at all," Danella refuted. "I just like being apprised of what's going on in my company."

"You're jealous because it's Lethia who's in the limelight and not you."

"I'm not," Danny howled indignantly, irritated because Logan could think her so petty. "However, I will admit that I'm worried. With all the opposition Lethia's giving me, I can't imagine her having been chosen as the media spokesperson for Blaketon Pharmaceuticals. I don't trust Lethia Blake, and I'm wondering what she'll say when her audience is a large metropolitan area, or the state, or the nation."

"The best thing you can do, Danella, is to forget it," Logan told her bruskly. "Publicity is *my* area of expertise, not *yours*. You salvage the company and manage it; I'll publicize Blaketon Pharmaceuticals. And put your mind at ease: I'll keep Lethia from saying anything that is damaging to the company. Now, if you're through, Ms. Jones . . ."

Before he could complete his sentence, short, rotund Ona Winfield opened the door, briskly moving to the large desk, placing two stacks of papers in front of Danella. She pointed to one. "These are the minutes and the directives, and"—her finger moved to the other stack—"these are the files you asked for. Each is complete; all that's needed is your signature. When you get through with them, I can start processing them."

Danella picked up the first file on the stack, idly thumbing through the neatly packaged pages. "I'll sign them right now, Ona, and you can have them ready for the mail Monday morning."

"Er . . ." Ona cleared her throat, her eyes traveling to the small digital clock on Danella's desk. "Can it wait until Monday, Ms. Jones? It's . . . it's quite late now."

Danella looked at the clock. Five-thirty! She slapped the file closed, lifting a hand to her forehead and apologizing, "I'm sorry, Ona. I didn't realize what time it was." She shook her head, rubbing her hand across her throbbing temples. "The meeting took much longer than I had anticipated."

"I know." Ona bobbed her head sympathetically. She smiled at Danella. "And I didn't mind staying. But I think we both ought to go home now. You just put these up and wait till Monday to read and sign them." She leaned over and patted Danella's shoulder. "You've had a pretty hard week, young lady. Go home and relax." She looked at Logan, and she grinned and winked. "Have a real good time this weekend." Then she turned,

54

marched out of the room, and closed the door behind her.

"I didn't realize it was so late," Danny said to Logan, picking up the files and dropping them into her briefcase.

"I agree with your secretary, Danella." Logan's voice softened with tender concern. "It's time for you to put your worries about Blaketon Pharmaceuticals aside and enjoy your weekend." He looked at his watch. "Let me take you out to dinner?"

"I'm sure Lethia would approve of a third wheel," Danella mused, walking to the clothes rack and taking her coat off the peg. Before she could slip it over her shoulders, however, Logan was behind her, taking it out of her hands and holding it for her.

"I'm just following her home to pick up some of the material I need for publicity. But even if she were going out to dinner with me, she wouldn't mind your joining us," he softly intoned. "She's really quite a gal when you get to know her."

"I'm sure I shall never know her as well as you do," Danella returned dryly, wiggling into her coat.

"Don't be so hard on her, Danella. She's an astute woman who can really help you. She's got a lot to give, if you'll just let her give it."

"Yeah, I know," Danny quipped without thinking, "she's been giving me plenty of trouble." Sorry the minute she uttered the words, Danella murmured her thanks and returned to her desk, opening the drawer and taking out her purse. Then she closed the lid of her briefcase, her hand closing over the handle.

Together, she and Logan walked through Ona's office just as Ona put her coat on. The secretary bustled out with them, talking about the weather, hoping she'd get home before the rain started. She wished Danella a good weekend, climbed into her car, and drove out of the parking lot and down the tree-lined asphalt lane that ran to the main road.

"Sure you won't change your mind?" Logan asked, walking Danella to her car and waving at Lethia, who sat in hers.

As Danella unlocked her car door, she shook her head. "Not tonight."

"See you around, then." Logan's words were lost in a blast of icy wind. Turning, he walked across the parking lot to Lethia, and Danella watched them, loneliness turning her eyes a dull gray. Unconsciously she thought about the steaks she'd bought to cook for herself and Brock. The salad. The cake that she had baked. The wine. She felt terribly alone.

Then a great gust of wind came billowing through the parking lot, whipping around her, pushing her against the car. She felt the drops of rain as they splattered on her face. Reaching up and brushing the hair out of her eyes, she quickly climbed into her car, revved the motor, and followed Logan's car along the long asphalt drive to the main highway.

By the time she reached her little house, the rain was falling in heavy sheets. She drove into the small detached garage and parked, glad for the short respite from the rain. She hunted through her purse for her keys before she darted out the side door, running for the back porch. As she reached the covering, however, her shoe caught between the flagstones and she fell down.

The pain that shot up her leg momentarily paralyzed her, and it was a few minutes before she could feel more than excruciating agony. Eventually she lifted her hands and pushed her wet hair out of her face, then shook her head, looking at her ruined stockings. She took off her shoes and examined them, hoping she hadn't stripped the leather off the heels.

Pushing herself to her feet, she picked up her purse and her briefcase, tucked them under an arm, and, clutching her shoes in her other hand, hobbled to the porch. Limping inside, she laid her paraphernalia on the breakfast table. Shivering, she made her way to the gas stove, turning on all the burners and the oven before she walked into the bathroom and lit the heater.

Because she had been so busy with the company, she hadn't taken the time to have the public utility service check her furnace; therefore it wasn't lit. So she'd have to make do with the stove, the bathroom heater, and the fireplace in the living room. While the bathroom was warming, she knelt in front of the cold, dark fireplace, breaking the kindling.

Once a bright fire was roaring, she painfully made her way to the bedroom and searched through drawers and the closet for warm, dry clothing. Then she scurried into the old-fashioned bathroom with its old-fashioned fixtures, the four-legged bathtub, the sink, and the toilet with its water reservoir mounted above it on the wall. The bathroom was probably her favorite room in the house, she thought as she dropped her wet clothing at her feet. She had immediately loved it and had enjoyed decorating it. Having a natural talent for decoration, she had designed the shower herself and had hired a plumber to install it.

Turning on the water, she stepped into the shower and pulled the curtain around the brass curtain rod, completely enclosing the tub. She welcomed the hot, steaming shower as she bathed. Quickly she dried off and combed her hair, shaking it around her face so that it would be fluffy when it was dry. She quickly put on her underwear, her thick flannel pajamas, and her heavy robe. Then she hung up her towel and washcloth and shuffled into the kitchen, her fleece-lined house shoes and socks in hand.

Mixing herself a vodka and orange juice, Danella returned to the living room, curled into a ball on the end of the sofa, and surveyed her house. If ever a house had her name on it, she felt as though this one did. It comprised a large living room, two bedrooms, one bath, a formal dining room, and a large old-fashioned kitchen with room for a breakfast table. The dining room was exceptionally beautiful, and she was proud of it and the way she had decorated it. She had found her table and chairs in a junkyard in Atlanta, and she had stripped them down to the natural wood herself. Then she had hunted for months before she found an old kitchen safe, a hutch, and a serving cart that complemented her table.

Danella stood, hobbled to the door of the dining room and looked at the table, which rested on a braided rug in blues and browns. Set for two, her dishes were a muted shade of blue with a beige design. A crystal wineglass stood by each plate, and the silverware was her grandmother's set. It was one of Danella's most prized possessions.

Danella set her empty glass on the floor. Catching the doorframe with both her hands, she laid her cheek against the cool parchment-colored woodwork. She had worked so hard, she thought, and Brock hadn't been able to come. She stared at the silver candle holders and then at the beige scented candles, and for a moment she thought she was going to cry.

She had spent long, grueling hours getting the house fixed up before Brock came for his first visit. She had wanted him to be as happy with it and as proud of it as she was. She had persuaded her landlady to let her paint the interior of the house herself instead of waiting for the painters; then she had driven to Wilmington on two occasions to shop for accessories, spending a small fortune on the country-ruffle drapes that hung in every window in the house. After that, her evenings had been devoted to unpacking and setting up the furniture. Her hands and knees were sore and calloused from her cleaning and waxing the hardwood floors.

Slowly she felt her strength ebb away, and her tears began to flow, as she gave vent to the loneliness, the disappointment, the despair, and the throbbing ache in her ankle. When finally the tears had subsided and the racking sobs had ended, Danella knelt and picked up her empty glass and slowly moved into the kitchen. After she prepared herself a quick TV dinner in the microwave, she ate. Then she filled a dishpan with hot salt water and carried it to the living room. She poured herself another drink. Sitting in the dim glow that radiated from the fire, she soaked her foot and listened to the rain as it pelted against the roof. As she sipped her drink she gazed at the beautiful red, gold, and orange flames that gracefully danced up the chimney.

Finally, when her foot was as wrinkled as a prune, she dried it off and limped into the bedroom, set the dial on her electric blanket, and crawled beneath the covers. But she didn't immediately turn off the lamp or nestle down. Instead she flipped over on her side, picked up the phone, and dialed. When she heard her father's deep voice on the line, she felt happy for the first time in hours.

"Danny!" Vernon Jones exclaimed. "What a surprise! How are things going?" Danella gave her father a quick rundown on her work. When he asked, "Spencer handling publicity for you?" he was traveling on the same path of memories as Danella, and he knew the answer before she said it.

"Yes." But Danella didn't add more. She was still smarting from the day's battle wounds, and she felt as if she'd been vanquished.

"I'm glad," her father said warmly. "I understand that he's one of the best."

"That's what Warrington's told you?" Danny didn't bother to hide her resentment.

"Yes, but Warrington's word isn't all I'm basing my

recommendation on. I've heard others speak of him and his work; I have confidence in his ability to get this off the ground. Whether you want to admit it or not, Danny, Logan's about the only guy around who can do it."

She knew her father was right, even though Danella didn't want to admit it. She somehow felt a sense of security in remembering the wild goose chase she believed he had led Jackie on five years earlier. And his siding with Lethia hadn't helped his image in her eyes at all.

"You've got to forget what happened," Vernon told her. "And you've got to realize that no matter what Jackie told you, it's not all Logan's fault. Remember, there are two sides to every story, and despite what you think, Danny, Jackie was not an emotionally strong woman. To the contrary, I think she was an exceptionally weak person. There are many things that could have driven her to take her own life. You and I can only guess at what they were."

After talking with her father and mother for a while, Danella switched off the light and snuggled under the covers. Now she could go to sleep. It was surprising how a few words with her parents could help her so much. They listened, they objectively analyzed, but they always left the final decision to Danella. Once she had talked with them, however, it was easier for her to put things in their proper perspective. She trusted their judgment.

Now she could find refuge in the peaceful oblivion of sleep. Tomorrow she would worry about Blaketon Pharmaceuticals. Tomorrow she would think about Lethia. And, she promised herself, tomorrow she *wouldn't* think about Logan Spencer. But no matter how hard she tried, she couldn't push Logan out of her thoughts. The last thing she remembered before she fell into a peaceful slumber was his face—those mischievous blue eyes, the unruly sandy waves that framed his face, the broken nose, the sensuous smile that so frequently curved those beautiful lips.

CHAPTER THREE

The following week Danella slowly hobbled around on her sprained ankle. But despite her physical handicap, she had won a major victory. At her insistence Horace Warrington had notified Logan that he was to be directly accountable to Danny, since she was the manager. But Danella didn't gloat over having made her point; she made concessions too. Being honest and practical, and trying to put the needs of the company before her personal biases, she agreed with Logan, telling Horace that Lethia was important to the company. She also told him that Lethia was an excellent choice as spokesperson.

A reassured Danny settled into the routine of running Blaketon Pharmaceuticals, and the weeks passed swiftly. When Logan was in Blaketon, he dropped by Danny's office to apprise her of his plans and to consult with her, but his visits were short and to the point, always concerning publicity. He never tried to push their relationship beyond professional friendliness. It seemed to Danella that he was more interested in being with Lethia, because he spent most of his free time with her.

When, at four o'clock on a Tuesday afternoon, Jane

Harris, a local newswoman in Wilmington, called Blaketon Pharmaceuticals, asking for an interview on the following Friday, Danella tentatively agreed. But, remembering her promise to Logan, she refused to give a final confirmation until she had conferred with him. She called Logan and asked him to come to her office to discuss the interview. Logan said he couldn't make it that day and suggested that they meet early the next morning at Danella's office.

But on Wednesday morning Danella's plans were again thwarted. Logan was called out of town on an emergency. When he returned, his secretary promised, he would call Danella that night at home. As much as Danella hated to admit it to herself, she was irritated and strangely disappointed. From the picture that Jackie had drawn of Logan, this wasn't the type of behavior she expected. She had thought he would try to push his way into her life.

But Logan wasn't playing the game of seduction at all, Danny thought a little later as she walked out of her office. Could it mean that he wasn't interested in her? That was not the way he had acted at first, she thought. And as much as she might pretend to find solace in the idea that he didn't appeal to her, Danny found herself disturbed by the prospect. She wondered what there was about her that he didn't like. Irritated, she inserted the key in the ignition and revved the motor a little harder than she needed to. The tires screeched as she inadvertently sped down the narrow road.

Driving home, she tried to concentrate on other things in order to get Logan off her mind, but she couldn't. His haunting presence angered her. But why should that be? she wondered. She had told him in no uncertain terms that she wanted to have as little to do with him as possible. Yet, she felt an inexplicable sense of loss when he was not around.

He was certainly different from most of the men she

knew. She had always preferred men she felt safe with—men like Brock. She could never be safe with a man like Logan Spencer, she knew. With him any woman was always at risk.

Slowly she walked across the flagstone to the back porch, unlocking the door and entering the kitchen. Glad that she had finally thought to have the public service board inspect her furnace, she switched it on. Then she walked to the bedroom, dropping her briefcase on the coffee table in the living room as she passed by. Had she allowed Jackie's experience with Logan to affect her this drastically? Had it become something of an obsession with her, one that colored her perceptions and prevented her from seeing things as they actually were?

Now that Danny thought about it, she realized her entire outlook had changed immediately after Jackie's suicide. She had changed overnight. She had begun to look disdainfully on men, promising herself that she would never let any man hurt her as much as Logan had hurt Jackie.

Danny took off her clothes and hung them up, thinking about the coming holiday. She had considered flying to Augusta to spend the day with her parents but had changed her mind, realistically opting to eat Thanksgiving dinner with her landlady, Bessie Faircloth, and Bessie's family. Because Bessie had talked so much about her two sons, their wives, and their children, Danny felt as if she knew all of them personally. In truth she had only met one daughter-in-law, Teresa, who was pregnant and the center of Bessie's immediate attention. Although the baby wasn't due for three more weeks, Bessie declared that it would be coming any day now.

"I can tell," the little woman had announced one day. "Just by the way it's dropped. And it's going to be another girl." She clicked her tongue. "I know Clyde and Terry want a boy after three girls, but . . ."

Chuckling as she recalled Bessie's prognostication, Danny quickly changed clothes. After she had dressed in faded jeans and a plaid shirt, she slowly wandered through the house at a loss for something to do. She didn't want to spend the evening cooped up at home; she didn't want to read or watch television; and she certainly didn't want to work. She wanted to go out, and she just might. Perhaps she'd drive up to Wilmington and do her shopping. But first she needed to take care of her empty stomach.

Before she prepared herself a light supper, she ran to the mailbox, happy when she found two letters from home, one from her mother and one from Brock. Laying them on the table, she quickly tossed a green salad, broiled a pork chop, and heated some leftover rice in the microwave, daubing a generous helping of butter onto the steaming mound. Pouring herself a goblet of chilled wine, she sat down to read and eat.

Saving Brock's letter for last, Danny opened her mother's. She enjoyed Ella's humorous account of the happenings at home so much that she reread the letter twice. Then she picked up Brock's. While his letter was light and newsy, Danella sensed the subtle change that distance was making in their relationship. He mentioned Amy Denvers several times, a fact that didn't please Danella at all. When Danny was through reading the letter, she slowly refolded it and put it back in the envelope. She knew that Brock's attention was certainly centered on Amy, and she wondered how long it would be before Brock also transferred his affection to Amy.

Pushing her empty plate away and pouring herself a second glass of wine, Danny sat back and leaned against the wall. She pulled her feet into the chair and hugged her arms around her legs, resting her chin on her knees. Lately she had found herself going for days without thinking about Brock. That was bad enough but what bothered her even more was that Logan Spencer seemed to have taken up permanent residence in her thoughts. Even as she sat there, determined not to think of that insufferable man, she couldn't help but wonder where Logan was tonight and what he was doing. Moreover, she wondered with whom he was doing it.

What kind of woman would it take to settle Logan Spencer down? she wondered, taking a sip of wine, savoring it, and swallowing slowly. As she pondered she cradled the wineglass in both hands and closed her eyes. Intuitively she knew that Logan would want more than just a body. He would want an intelligent woman, one who could hold her own in a conversation. He would want a woman who could meet with the public, who could handle herself no matter what the situation. Unbidden, the image of Lethia Blake came to Danella's mind. Did he prefer the sophisticated gentility of Lethia Blake? Did he prefer an older woman? After all, Lethia was the one whom he had chosen to be the spokesperson for Blaketon Pharmaceuticals. She was the one with whom he preferred to spend most of his time.

The thought of Lethia shattered Danella's beautiful dreams. Standing, she picked up her plate and flatware and carried them to the sink, rinsing them before she stacked them in the dishwasher. Then she carried her half-filled glass of wine into the living room. Turning the lamp on low beam, she curled up on the end of the couch, pushing Lethia's image aside, letting Logan freely consume her thoughts, gladly returning to the hazy, warm world of her dreams. If just working with Logan had this effect on her, she could only imagine what going out with him would be like.

An enchanting smile played on her feminine lips, which glistened evocatively with droplets of sparkling wine. She recalled his inviting her to dance the first night they met. Allowing her fancy to fly, Danella could see herself on the dance floor; she could feel his arms around her as he held close, as he stroked her. He was one of those men who was altogether masculine, the kind of man who would go out of his way to make an evening enjoyable for a woman.

He would be an exciting date—those beautiful blue eyes; those firm lips; that beguiling smile, capable of turning friendliness into intimacy in a second; the grazing touch of those hands. Danny imagined his male attentiveness; the slow, deliberate, and careful seduction of her senses; his expert guidance and tutorage in the splendors of lovemaking. Danny smiled and stretched sinuously, her thoughts totally captivating and exciting. She tried to imagine what a relationship between them would be like. It would be primeval—a skirmish of wills that slowly merged into a battle of the minds, finally resulting in that age-old battle of the sexes, that never-ending struggle for dominance. It could be no less between her and Logan.

The sound of a car braking in the driveway jostled Danny back to the cold reality of her living room. Rising, she walked across the floor and flipped the switch, bathing the room in the harsh glare of overhead light. Why was she daydreaming about making love to Logan Spencer? she wondered. How could she even think such traitorous thoughts? *Remember what he did to Jackie, Danella Jones!* she thought. *Remember what happened after she surrendered to him. Remember what happened when their affair ended! So did Jackie's life!*

Pushing the curtain aside, Danella looked through the beveled glass panes into the gray-shadowed dusk that was settling on the small community. She couldn't believe her eyes. The man, the physical expression of her daydreams, was strolling across her lawn, softly whistling as if he hadn't a care in the world. His sudden presence jarred her from the warm security of make-believe. The soft, tremulous smile disappeared from her lips, and her eyes narrowed in wary apprehension.

What was he doing there? What did he want? As the questions flew around in her mind like the fluttering of autumn leaves in a great gust of wind, Danny's hand automatically closed over the brass knob. She twisted and pulled open the large door, moving to stand in the aperture as if to block his entrance. Logan's head lifted at the sound, and he raised a hand and waved. Although Danny returned the gesture, she was flabbergasted. This was the last person in the world whom she had expected to see this evening.

"And to what do I owe the honor?" Danny's husky contralto was still affected by her daydreams.

The whistling stopped as Logan lithely sprinted up the steps and dropped his hands to his hips in his familiar athletic stance. "What if I said I just happened to be passing by?"

"I wouldn't believe you."

Logan's lips gently curved into a mocking smile, and he laughed softly. "So young to be so skeptical, Ms. Jones."

"Not skeptical," Danny corrected, "just wary of wolves dressed in sheep's clothing."

Logan lifted his hands, protesting his innocence. "Neither a wolf nor a sheep. Just a man." As he said the words his eyes, warm and sensual, slowly traveled the length of her slim body. "Just a man who happened to want to see a certain beautiful woman." His gaze continued to lower as he made a very careful assessment of the feminine curves that were revealed and enhanced by her faded jeans and buttoned plaid shirt.

Danny tried to retreat from the intimacy of his words and his gaze, but she felt her cheeks flush with warm pleasure as his eyes finally came to rest on the opening of her shirt.

"You were supposed to call me."

68

"I did, but your line has been busy all afternoon." Mundane words, nothing more. Only an answer to a question. Yet, Logan's reply was velvety smooth, touching all of Danny's nerve endings, making them tingle with anticipation and desire.

She looked at him questioningly, wrinkling her forehead. "That couldn't be. I haven't been talking."

Logan chuckled softly, and his blue eyes twinkled wickedly. "I'll just bet that you're on a party line, Danny girl."

Danny began to smile, but she quickly caught herself. "I forgot," she exclaimed softly. "I had to take a party line temporarily, and"—she chuckled—"I'm sharing the line with my landlady, who's quite a talker. More so now than ever before."

Logan lifted his thick brows.

"Her daughter-in-law Teresa is expecting a baby in about three weeks, but Bessie declares that it'll be any day now."

Unable to resist, Danny mimicked Bessie's latest report on Teresa's condition, inadvertently introducing Logan to the Faircloths one by one. Not really interested in Danny's landlady or her family but totally engrossed in Danella Jones, Logan laughed with her, watching her changing expressions as she spoke and listening to the rising and falling inflections of her voice.

Danella was so occupied with recounting Bessie Faircloth's saga that it wasn't until she stopped talking that she realized that Logan was staring at her. His face hid none of his inner feelings. Ducking her head to avoid his intent gaze, she murmured, "Enough of this. Come on in. We've got more important things to do than stand on the porch and discuss party lines, pregnant women, and landladies."

Logan grinned, indolently reaching out to tuck an errant strand of hair behind Danny's ear. "I can think of one thing I would like right now." Danny drew her

69

breath in sharply, and like the deep slice of a knife the pain seared through her chest. "I'm dead tired, hungry, and thirsty," Logan continued. "I sure could use a cup of hot coffee, if you have one." He paused, letting his confession sink in, silently smiling at the telltale color that spread across Danny's countenance, blatantly revealing that she had expected him to say something quite different.

Danella slowly expelled the air from her lungs. Then she laughed and tossed her head, her beautiful hair swirling around her face. "I think that can be arranged. If you'd like, I could fix you something to eat."

"Sounds like a winner," he told her, brushing past her and moving into the living room.

He quickly took off his jacket, handed it to her, and waited in the living room while she hung it up. When Danny returned from the bedroom, he followed her into the kitchen. While she busied herself with the meal, he pulled a chair from the table and sat down, stretching his legs in front of himself. He rolled up his sleeves and lifted his arms, locking both hands at the nape of his neck. Then he watched as she measured the grounds and filled the coffee maker with water. Contentedly he watched her take a pork chop from the refrigerator and drop it in the broiler. Sighing deeply, he relaxed, and after a while he closed his eyes. It wasn't until Danella set a cup of steaming coffee in front of him that he moved.

As if it took great effort, he hunched over the table, reaching for the sugar bowl. "I stopped by Lethia's on the way over here."

Always Lethia, Danny thought irritably. Without a word she returned to the counter, her back to Logan.

"Just a little bit more and we'll have the history of Blake House and Blaketon Pharmaceuticals finished." Danny heard Logan's spoon as it clinked against the side of the sugar bowl. "I couldn't have done it without her, Danny. She's really been a great help."

Danny speared the pork chop with a vengeance and turned it over before she walked to the refrigerator, taking out some lettuce, tomatoes, and salad dressing. "I'm sure she has. The two of you have really been working closely together." Although Danny didn't intend it to be, her answer was curt, a note that sounded suspiciously like jealousy running through her voice.

Logan stopped stirring his coffee, lifted his head, and peered at Danny, grinning. "If it bothers you, Danny girl, that I'm working so closely with Lethia Blake, I'm open for an offer."

As if she were pouncing on a deadly snake, Danny jabbed the pork chop one last time and dropped it on Logan's plate. "It doesn't bother me at all, and I never make bids on such things."

"I'm open for some loving persuasion."

Logan's quiet chuckle burrowed under Danny's skin, pricking her with an acute awareness of the man, stimulating feelings she didn't know she possessed, whetting desires she didn't know if she could handle. Not deigning to answer, Danella spun around and carried him his dinner. She sat opposite him in silence and watched as he began to attack it voraciously.

"Ummm," Logan murmured, swallowing his first bite of food. "This is good." He shoveled his fork a second time into the steaming mound of buttered rice. "Not many people know how to cook rice like this, so it's not thick and pasty."

"Thank you."

"Not only are you a highly qualified managerial and developmental consultant, Ms. Danella Jones, you are also a good cook."

"Again, thank you." Happy with his compliments in spite of herself, Danny's answer was flavored with a smile. "But in all honesty, it doesn't take too much ability to brew coffee, broil a pork chop, toss salad, and reheat rice."

"Not much," Logan conceded softly, lifting the coffee cup to his lips.

All the while, however, he looked intently at Danny, visually touching her slightly tousled hair, her creamy cheeks, the contours of her lips. Finally, after what seemed to Danny to be hours, Logan's gaze slipped to the satiny flesh that peeked enticingly above the V of her shirt. They lingered appreciatively before they slowly moved upward.

"But you definitely have what it takes, Danny, and I have a feeling that you are good at anything you do."

The soft promise whispered over Danella, and she shivered. Breaking the visual bond between them, she lowered her eyes, running her finger around the rim of her glass. She forced herself to breathe normally; she willed her accelerated heartbeat to slow down. She couldn't allow herself to become ensnared in his trap. She wouldn't give in to the charm of this man.

Logan, totally intrigued by the woman who sat across from him, allowed the tip of his tongue to rest on his smiling lips. She wasn't as unaffected by him as she wanted him to think, he realized. He reached across the table and took her hand in his, stilling its nervous movement as he gently squeezed.

"Danny, for what it's worth, I've only been working with Lethia. There's nothing personal about our seeing one another, and we're in no way conspiring against you." He paused, adding softly, "It's not a personal interest for either one of us."

Danny kept her head lowered, but she didn't pull her hand from his firm grip. Rather, she relaxed, letting the tension flow out of her body as Logan's warmth and strength replaced it. "That's"—she moistened her dry lips with her tongue—"that's what you said about you and Jackie."

72

"And it's the truth in both instances," he insisted without raising his voice. "Jackie was an insecure woman who evidently couldn't handle her own emotions, and she let her fantasies overshadow reality until they became her reality."

Danella just stared at him questioningly.

Logan shook his head and continued, "Lethia is just very insecure about the takeover, but that's only normal. Now that Warrington has bought the company and her position company- and communitywise has been reestablished, she'll stand on her own two feet. She's totally dedicated to being a Blake and to all that being a Blake entails." He chuckled. "And I know that Lethia has no time for amorous attractions." He reached across the table to touch Danny's chin with the tips of his fingers, lifting her face. "Do you believe me?"

Unable to meet his penetrating eyes but also unable to avert her face, Danny looked downward, her gaze hungrily moving along the column of his strong, tan throat, down to the patch of sandy hair that was revealed at the open neck of his shirt. Suddenly she wanted to bolt and run, to flee his presence. She could handle him in her imagination, but he was too much for her in reality. Maybe she was like Jackie. Perhaps fantasy was easier for her to accept than reality.

"Please believe me, Danny." His voice, though soft, was not a whisper, and Danella could hear the quiet supplication.

She wanted to believe him—really she did! But she felt all her fears resurfacing; she could feel Jackie between them. Yet, new feelings were rivaling the hatred and fear that Jackie had instilled in Danella. Those new emotions were slowly and surely surpassing doubt and question.

"I—I think I do," she replied unevenly.

"Danny, I—"

73

"Not now, Logan. No more, please." Those soft gray eyes locked with his; she pleaded with him.

After a moment's hesitation he nodded. "Okay." His voice lowered to a seductive level. "For now."

Breaking the magic of the moment, Danny pulled her hand out of his grasp, picked up the dishes, and carried them to the sink. Understanding her need for some space, Logan stood and walked to the cabinet, taking out a second goblet. He opened the refrigerator and filled both glasses with wine. Leaning one shoulder against the refrigerator, he watched her as she worked.

"Got your turkey day planned?" The question was casual, but his query was serious; it was calculated.

Thinking about both her landlady and her briefcase full of work, Danny nodded and managed a smile. "Yes," she said. "It's going to be quite full."

"Big dinner?" He looked at the goblet he held in his hand, pretending more interest in his wine than in her.

"Yes, my landlady has invited me to have dinner with her." Danny closed the door of the dishwasher and wrung out her dish towel.

"Sounds like you're taken care of, then."

"I am. What about you?" She walked onto the enclosed back porch to hang the damp cloth on the rack to dry. "Planning on going home?"

"Nope. Gotta work," he said succinctly, quickly dropping the subject. "And speaking of work, let's discuss this interview you've got with Jane Harris." He lifted his arm and glanced at his watch. "I have to shove off pretty soon." He picked up her glass of wine. "I'm gonna be cooking the big *T* tomorrow. Thanksgiving is on me this year."

"You!" Danny laughed. "You're going to cook your own Thanksgiving dinner?"

"I certainly am!" Logan feigned indignation. "I am a very good cook."

"If you say so," Danny retorted, leading the way into

the living room to the forgotten briefcase on the coffee table.

"If you'll have dinner with me tomorrow," Logan dared her, "I'll prove to you how good a cook I am."

The melodious sound of Danny's laughter resounded through the room. Shaking her head, she said, "I think I want to live a little longer—at least until I get Blaketon Pharmaceuticals on its feet." Setting her glass of wine down as she sat on the edge of the sofa, she opened the case and pulled out the notes she had jotted down when Jane had called. Briefly she gave him a summary of her conversation with the reporter. "She wants to concentrate on Blake's new image." When Danny handed Logan the sheet of paper, she stood, walking to the window. "The old versus the new."

Setting lazily into the softness of the sofa cushions, Logan sipped his wine and read Danella's notes. Finally he said, "Danella Jones versus Liston Blake."

"No," Danny stated, her back to him, her voice softly carrying across the room. "Danella Jones versus Lethia Blake."

Logan heard the words. He heard more: He heard Danny's fears, her doubts, and her questions. Setting his glass on the table and letting the sheet of paper flutter to the floor without a second thought, Logan stood and covered the distance that separated them, stopping immediately behind her.

"It's not really Danella Jones versus Lethia Blake."

The softness and the gentleness of his words disconcerted Danella, and they acted like a key to open the floodgate to her unhappiness. Unchecked, it poured out.

"Yes it is. Jane didn't say it, but I could feel it. She's a Blaketonian even though she lives in Charlotte and writes for the paper there. She was nice, but I could feel the subtle tension that existed between us."

Logan's big hands settled gently on Danny's shoulders,

and they began to knead the tense muscles, moving to the nape of her neck and back to her shoulders. "You're making too much out of this."

Danny shrugged, letting herself relax beneath his touch. "Not really. And it's not just Jane Harris. I met with the two men who were asking for transfers, and I've used all my arguments to stop them. They're still determined to go." She paused for a second. "I thought if Lethia would talk to them, she could change their minds, but she refuses."

"So you may lose them," he softly consoled. "It's not the end of the world—just an unexpected port of call. You'll find someone just as qualified to replace them. It may take you a little longer than you had projected. It'll just slow you down, but it certainly won't stop you."

"I know," she murmured, sighing, releasing her disappointment, giving in to the pleasure of his hands as they tenderly pressed into the taut flesh of her shoulders and neck. They stood for a long time before Danny asked, "Logan, how much longer do you think Lethia will continue to fight me?"

"Not long," he replied. "Her fighting is about over with. And it wasn't you per se that she was fighting, Danny love." The endearment slipped unconsciously from his lips. "She was just running scared from the changes that Warrington's takeover would effect. You became the symbol of all those changes, and thus the focal point of her bitterness and animosities."

"Scared of me!" Danny exclaimed, spinning around to confront him with the absurdity of his words.

"You," Logan quietly refuted. "You're so young, so determined, and so confident."

"Oh, Logan," Danny wailed, "that's the way I see *her*, not *myself*. I've never been as unsure of myself as I am right now."

He chuckled. "No one could tell that by looking at and listening to you. You can be mighty haughty and condescending, young lady. You even scare me sometimes when you're cracking your whip."

Danny laughed. "Now that's an outright lie, Logan Spencer. I know you're not afraid of me. And I strongly doubt that Lethia or anyone else is." She pushed her hand through her hair. "I don't know if I can win against a martyr or not, Logan, and that's exactly what Lethia Blake is. These people revere her. She can do no wrong, and I can do no right."

"Sure you can. You've just got to move slowly. You're not going to be able to make all your changes immediately."

"But I must make changes or the company will be a failure," Danella swore softly. "I've got to, Logan." Her voice dropped to an agonizing whisper. "And Lethia and the people have got to realize that these changes are for the betterment, not the detriment, of the company and the employees."

"You'll make your changes," he agreed, smiling confidently, never having doubted her ability. "If you'll give Lethia and the community time, they'll come around. I think that in time, you and Lethia will become great friends."

Danny nodded, but Logan could tell that she didn't believe him. "Come on," he told her, putting his arm around her shoulder and guiding her to the sofa. "It's going to be all right. Let's discuss this interview." Returning to the sofa, they sat down. "Have you ever done one before?" Danny shook her head. "I thought not. First thing we'll have to do is reschedule. The day after tomorrow is too soon," he mused. "Give me her phone number and I'll get us a date for the following week."

Feeling that Logan wanted to take control of the situation, Danny said, "I don't want it rescheduled. The Friday after Thanksgiving is an excellent time for me."

Leaning forward, Logan reached for a note pad. "I

don't think you're in a proper emotional state to handle the interview."

Danny's eyes opened wide. "What do you mean?" she asked indignantly.

Logan dropped his pencil and pad and reached for her hands. "Danny, the press can be merciless as well as arbitrary. You must be very careful."

"And you think I'll say something that will reflect badly on the company—or Lethia?" she demanded.

"No, I'm afraid that you'll say something that will reflect badly on you." His grasp tightened, and he gently shoved her into the softness of the cushions, willing her to relax and to listen to him. "In all fairness to Jane, I'm not intimating that she will deliberately misquote you, but in print, Danny—in black and white— words tend to take on different meanings from the ones you originally intended. A reporter can't print every word that you utter, so she's going to have to use her judgment and pick what she thinks will be the most informative for the public. And those words on paper will not have inflections to alert people to your meanings; there will be no warmth or smiles to soften their harshness. Therefore you must weigh each word that you say." He smiled and paused, letting the significance of his words sink in. "I don't mind when you give the interview: It is, after all, your business. But I would like to give you support. Since I've got to be in Raleigh on Friday, I can't be with you. If we reschedule, I can be."

Danny saw a facet of Logan's personality that she had never known to exist. He truly seemed to want to protect her; he was thinking about her. She nodded, her anger and disappointment evaporating. Reaching into her briefcase, she opened her small address book and read off Jane's number.

After Logan had jotted it down on his pad, he tore off the sheet, folded the paper into a small square, and tucked it into his pocket. Then they sat back on the sofa in the dim glow that radiated from the fire, quietly listening to the autumn wind that blew through the trees and huffed around the house. They sipped their wine and gazed at the beautiful flames in the fireplace.

Finally, Logan rose and looked at his watch. "It's late. I'd better get going. I've still got a drive ahead of me."

Hating to see him go but having no plausible reason for detaining him, Danny said, "I'm glad you came."

"Have dinner with me tomorrow, Danny?"

"I've already promised Bessie."

"What about going out tomorrow night?"

"Can't," she said, knowing her answer sounded lame, but there was no place in her personal life for Logan Spencer—especially now that she was finding him so attractive. He was too dangerous. "I've got loads of work to do in preparation for the conference this weekend."

"If that's the way you want it . . . ."

Even though he sounded unconcerned, his words were a gentle reprimand. Naturally he wanted her to go out with him, but he wasn't going to beg her. Nor was he going to push her too fast. That could very easily backfire. With Danella Jones he had to move slowly and carefully.

"If you'll just get my coat . . ."

Danella stood, moving down the hall to the bedroom across from hers. Logan followed. She switched on the light and walked to the closet. When she returned to the door, Logan took the coat, but he made no effort to move. Rather, he stood, peering over her shoulder, looking at the white provincial furniture with its pink-and-white—ruffled accessories.

"It's definitely a little-girl's room."

"My furniture," she declared with a certain amount of love and pride, striving to keep her voice even and smooth, wishing Logan would move. His closeness was nerve-shattering, to say the least. "Mom and Dad let me have it for my spare bedroom."

"For their little girl." Logan's warm, wine-scented murmur touched her neck, blowing strands of her hair, swirling them around her cheeks and her throat.

"For their little girl who has grown into a woman," Danny whispered.

"For the scene to be complete, the woman needs a man."

"And I suppose you'll furnish the man."

"More than happy to," he whispered, leaning closer to her, his lips brushing against the top of her head. "Any takers?"

"I—I don't think so," she said softly, the wine having melted her wall of defenses. There was nothing standing between her and Logan Spencer. Nothing at all!

"Why not?" Logan asked. "Trust me. That's all I ask of you."

"I . . . I can't *ever* trust you, Logan," Danella answered, nearly choking on the words. "I saw the results of Jackie's loving you. I'm never going to let you hurt me as much as you hurt her."

"You still believe that?" Although he was puzzled, he kept his voice low. "After having known me all this time, you still see me through the distorted lens of someone else's eyes?"

"It's your word against hers."

"That's right," he concurred, his expression turning icy. "My word against hers." He watched Danella as she wrestled with his confession. "You're going to have to decide which one of us you really believe. It's going to be a tough decision for you to make, but only you can do it." He smiled at her. "I'm hoping that you'll believe me, that eventually you'll learn to trust me."

"Why?" Danella asked, lifting a hand to brush her hair away from her temples.

"Because I can very easily fall in love with you, Danella Jones. Ever since I met you—when fate literally swept you into my arms—I've been wondering what it would be like to hold you in my arms and to kiss you." His face came nearer and nearer to hers, his eyes midnight blue, dark and mysterious, mesmerizing her with their beauty and the hint of promise. "I haven't been able to get you out of my mind, Danny girl."

"No, Logan." Did that weak, ineffective voice belong to her?

"Yes," he whispered, his jacket falling to the floor, his hands cupping her chin and her neck, his thumbs stroking the sensitive fullness of her lips. "I've got to do it, Danny. I wish you trusted me, because it would make it better. But I'm going to kiss you anyway."

She knew she shouldn't let him hold her like that; she knew that she should avoid the kiss. But all the time her arms were entwining behind his head, locking around the nape of his neck.

Torn between conflicting emotions, Danella didn't allow herself to think about Jackie; she forgot what kind of lover Logan was reputed to be; she forgot the kind of heartaches he had caused. Willingly she waded into the water of desire that gently lapped at her feet, knowing that at any moment the floodgate could be released and she could be inundated in a torrential tide of passion.

"You taste so good, my darling."

His lips barely moved against hers, just a soft, undemanding brush of the mouth. At the touch, Danny felt a white-hot flash of lightning as it bolted through her soul. She tensed and pulled back, her eyes wide with astonishment. Then she saw the same amazement reflected in his eyes.

"No, Logan." This time she backed up her words with action, dropping her hands to his chest, trying to push herself out of his arms.

Danella's protest was lost as his lips played with hers,

hungrily devouring her resistance. Determinedly he concentrated on loving her. His arms tightened around her, and his lips began a thorough search of hers. He tasted her mouth as if it were a delicate morsel of food. He ran his tongue over her lips, seeking entrance between them. When his mouth finally settled on hers, one hand cupped the back of her head, the other slipped down her back to rest on her buttocks. He pulled her lower body closer to his as his lips moved in sensual rhythm against hers, ultimately evoking a response from the depth of her soul. Her mouth, obeying all his injunctions, opened fully beneath the pressure of his, allowing his tongue to sweep into the warm moistness, whetting her desires with each brushlike stroke.

When finally he lifted his lips from hers, Danny collapsed against his chest, turning her face, resting her cheeks on the soft, pale blue material. She dropped her arms, wrapping them around his torso, tenderly rubbing her hands up and down his back. They stood for the longest time before Logan spoke.

"Spend the day with me tomorrow, Danny?"

"No."

Although the word was no more than a whisper, there was no hesitation in its utterance. If only his kiss had touched the deepest part of her soul, what would more intimate caresses do to her. She couldn't afford to become another victim of Logan Spencer's charm. And whether Logan knew it or not, Jackie Wesson had been deeply in love with him. And whether it was intentional on his part or not, Jackie had not recovered from the devastating effects of her love for him. Danella Jones knew she couldn't afford Logan Spencer's love.

Unable to leave her, Logan gave voice to thoughts that surprised him as much as they surprised Danella. "Will you go grocery shopping with me?"

"Will I go grocery shopping with you?"

Danny softly mimicked the words, pulling back and

looking at him in happy surprise. Momentarily, she forgot that she hated grocery shopping and never went unless she absolutely had to. Momentarily she forgot her fears of Logan Spencer. She laughed, releasing the joy of her soul. "You want me to come grocery shopping with you?"

Logan nodded. "I'm a procrastinator when it comes to shopping, Danny. I always save everything for the last minute. I sure could use a woman's know-how." While he waited for her answer, he bent and picked up his jacket, slipping into it.

Danny's lips curved gently into a smile as bright as early-morning sunshine in spring. "Let me get my purse and lock the door. I'd love to come. I need to get a few things myself."

She scampered through the house, putting on a hint of lipstick, brushing her hair, changing shoes, and grabbing a heavy jacket from the closet. When they were seated in the car, she asked, "What are you going shopping for?"

"Everything."

"That's quite a lot."

"The cupboard's bare." He turned his face and looked at her, smiling whimsically, mysteriously. His hand snaked across the seat and caught hers in a warm, tight grasp. "Shall I tell you what else is bare, Danny?" When she didn't answer—when she *couldn't* answer—he said his voice low and sensuous, "What if I said my heart was bare and empty?"

Danny shrugged as if the physical action could dispel the intimacy with which his words cloaked her.

"What if I said that I'm interested in your filling my heart?"

"If I were sure that filling your heart was your primary purpose," Danny replied, her voice low, "perhaps I would give it some consideration. But I won't be another trophy for your wall."

"I see, Ms. Jones, that I have a lot of persuading ahead of me." He chuckled, exhilarated at the challenge. "A lot of loving persuasion."

No man has succeeded in reaching my heart yet, Danny thought, frightened because Logan Spencer was at her heart's door that very minute, frightened because she had unlocked the door for him to enter. All he had to do was turn the knob and gently shove. She leaned back in her seat and looked out the window. Again understanding her need for space, Logan concentrated on his driving, finally turning off Main Street into the parking lot of the supermarket. He stopped the car, put it into park, and turned the motor off. Then he opened the door and slid from under the steering wheel. By the time he rounded the front of the car, Danny had emerged and they quietly walked into the supermarket. Then, with a familiar oneness, as if they had done this a thousand times, they began to shop for Logan's Thanksgiving dinner.

They went through the bins, searching for the right turkey. They lifted, they patted, they weighed, finally selecting one. They bought a small ham, sweet potatoes, and coarsely ground corn meal for dressing. With care they chose the green onions, the celery, the seasonings. Carefully they selected their frozen foods and their canned goods. From one end of the store to the other they rolled the shopping cart, and never before had Danella enjoyed buying groceries more; never had she bantered more or laughed more freely.

When they arrived at her house, Logan flicked off the headlights and grabbed Danny, pulling her across the seat before she could open her door and get out. Circling her waist with his arm, he tugged her out of the car and walked her to the porch. When she tried to twist out of his grip, his fingers became like manacles, entrapping her.

Standing on the front porch, Danny reached into her

jacket pocket and pulled out her key ring. Taking it from her, Logan unlocked and opened the door. He walked to the end table and turned on a lamp, letting the soft glow spill into the room. Then he checked each room in the house and returned to the living room, where Danny remained next to the door.

"No burglars," he told her. "Do I get a reward for my fearless protection?"

"What do you have in mind?" she asked, and then prayed he wouldn't answer her.

"I'll settle for a good-night kiss right now, Danny girl, but later . . ." The soft timbre of his whisper played on her nerves.

She smiled, pushing wisps of hair from around her face. "Not tonight." Her eyes twinkled, and her lips shimmered with a glowing smile. "I'm not that kind of girl."

And although her words were said in gentle jest, she meant them. It might be just a good-night kiss for Logan, but she knew without a doubt that for her it was a matter of the heart, a matter of life and death. If she allowed him to kiss her again, she would be paving the way for him to make love to her. To protect herself, she couldn't allow it to go further.

"You are my kind of girl, Danny."

Dear Lord, she thought, her nickname had never sounded so beautiful.

"I'm just as vulnerable as you are at this moment." He moved to where she stood, denying her any space, but he didn't touch her.

His words were as drugging and as alluring as his lovemaking, and Danny could feel the strength of his charm and temptation. She wanted to give in, to let him kiss her, to let him take her to the lofty heights of fulfillment.

Sensing her submission, he said, "You're affecting

me, too." His words were a growl of pleasure, and his body quivered with desire.

But Danny would not become a victim to her vulnerability as Jackie had done. She would resist Logan's loving persuasion. "Any woman would do," she whispered trying unsuccessfully to sound harsh. "I don't think you've done without for the past thirty-four years."

"I've had women, Danny, but I've never had love." The declaration hung for long seconds between them before Logan added, "And that's what I'm looking for. In all honesty, I meant what I said earlier. I'm lonely; my heart is bare."

Danny's tongue darted out and touched her parched lips. "I—I think it's time for you to be going, Logan."

"I don't think so," he replied, his eyes hungrily drinking their fill, committing to memory every centimeter of her face. "But I will."

He reluctantly turned, and his hand closed over the doorknob. He twisted it but he didn't immediately open the door; instead he stood staring into her face.

"Danny, for what it's worth, you're tearing me apart. Because you're a desirable woman, I want to love you." He lifted a hand and gently pushed the hair from her face. "Because I can see the little girl in you, I want to hold you tight." His eyes, deep and intense, gazed at her, searching into her soul. "I want to protect you from the world. Even more, I would like to share with you—your pain, your worries, your joys." His fingertips grazed her soft cheek. "I'd like to kiss you again." His thumb traced back and forth along her full bottom lip. "But more than that, I'd like to take you to bed and make love to you."

Mesmerized, Danella shook her head; however, with each word that he uttered, she felt herself capitulating. If he didn't hurry up and leave . . .

He paused, looking at her sincerely. "Most important, Danny, I'm not going to do any of these in an effort to convince you of my motives." He smiled. "Please come spend Thanksgiving with me."

"I—I can't disappoint Mrs. Faircloth," she muttered.

"But you can disappoint me?"

Danny stared at him, without uttering a word; however, her eyes betrayed her.

"I think you really want to, Danny. But I think you're still afraid."

Danny shook her head, but she knew he didn't believe her. She mumbled, "You'll call and let me know when you've rescheduled the interview?"

"I will."

"I guess I'll see you . . . at the interview, then."

"If not sooner," he promised.

CHAPTER FOUR

It wasn't until the second ring of the phone that Danella woke up and rolled over in the bed, not quite sure what had awakened her. She lay still for just a second, trying to get her bearings. Then she heard it again. She propped herself up on one elbow as her hand thrashed wildly around the nightstand. Finally she pressed the receiver to her ear and mumbled "Hello" into the mouthpiece.

"Danella, this is Bessie. Sorry to awaken you this early. . . ."

Danny sat bolt upright, switched on the light, and looked at the clock. It was five A.M.!

"I told you," Bessie's voice sang through the receiver. "Clyde just called. Teresa's in the hospital in labor."

"So the baby's coming early." Danny lay back down and yawned, happy for Teresa and Clyde but wishing Bessie had waited a few hours to tell her.

"Just as I thought," Bessie announced triumphantly, her voice quivering with excitement. "The doctor said three weeks, but I could tell by the position . . ." Danny listened through Bessie's blow-by-blow description of everything that had happened since Teresa had awakened Clyde and announced that she was in labor. Finally, Bessie concluded with "And mark my words, it's going to be another girl." Without pausing for breath, Bessie suddenly said, "I wanted to call to let you know that our plans haven't changed that much. Instead of my cooking dinner here, Jerry, my other son, is on his way down to get me now so I can stay with Clyde and Teresa's children."

Danny chuckled. "Thanks for calling, Bessie, and don't mind me. Junior certainly didn't."

"But that's just it," Bessie told her. "I'm calling because I want you to come with me."

"Thanks, but I've got so much work to do, Bessie, I'll just stay here. With the baby's arrival, things are going to be different. I know that you'll want to be at the hospital as much as possible."

"I don't want you to spend the day by yourself," Bessie howled. "Holidays are family days."

"Well . . ." Danny murmured, not knowing what to say but feeling certain she didn't want to impose on Bessie's family by going to their home for dinner.

"Tell you what," Bessie cried with sudden inspiration. "I'll give you Jerry's address and phone number. That way you can drive up later if you decide you want to."

After Bessie hung up, Danny jumped up and scurried through the house, turning on the furnace so the house would be warm when she got up. Then she hopped back into bed and switched off the lamp. She balled her hand into a fist and fluffed her pillow, snuggling into the warmth of her electric blanket. But she didn't soon drop off to sleep.

Instead her thoughts drifted to Logan. She remembered the touch of his lips on hers, the feel of his hands as they caressed her body. Letting the delicious memories wash over her, Danella curled into a ball, wondering what it would feel like to have Logan make love to her. . . .

*   *   *

It was late when the incessant pounding on her front door finally awakened Danella. Grumbling, she crawled out of bed and sleepily donned her bathrobe, and her fleece-lined house shoes. Barely awake, she shuffled to the door, wondering who it could be. When she opened the door and saw her visitor, her jaw dropped. Her surprise yesterday at having seen Logan was nothing in comparison to this morning.

"It took you long enough," he said, smiling at her startled expression. Logan, dressed in jeans and jacket, indolently lounged against the doorjamb, the brisk wind whipping his hair around his face.

"What are you doing here?" Danella gasped, her voice so raspy with sleep that her words were a mere grating sound.

"Came to get you." Logan pulling the screen door open, shoved on the wooden front door, pushing past Danella. "And if you don't mind, I'll come in. You can't expect me to stand on the front porch while I wait for you to dress."

"Dress?" Danny repeated, still bemused. "Dress for what?"

"Dress for me."

"That'll be the day." She grimaced. "What time is it anyway, and what are you doing here? Is there some emergency at work?" she asked, combing her fingers through her hair.

"It's ten-thirty, so hurry up. And no, there's no emergency."

"I'm not one to hurry before I have my first cup of coffee," she retorted, shuffling into the kitchen and filling the container with water. "I need at least one cup before I'm good for anything," she called over her shoulder as she opened the microwave and set the container inside. "Now, Logan, I want to know exactly what you're doing here."

90

Logan, having taken the time to shed his jacket, stood in the kitchen doorway, leaning against the jamb, his arms folded across his chest. His deep chuckle echoed through the small kitchen. "I have a feeling that you're good for quite a few things with or without your morning cup of coffee, Ms. Jones." Not waiting for a response but watching the robe that enticingly cupped her bottom when she stretched her arms to get the cups from the cabinet, Logan added, "And while you're at it, you can fix me a cup too."

Muttering to herself, Danella set the cups on the counter. She opened a bottom door and extracted the small jar of instant coffee. As she measured she asked, "Now the truth before I throw you out. What brings you down this way?"

"As I said before, I came to get you."

Danny didn't bother to set the jar down as she peered over her shoulder at him. She stared for a long time before she turned her head and replaced the cover of the jar. Without speaking, she put the coffee on the shelf and closed the cabinet door.

"I told you last night that I'm spending the day with my landlady and her family."

Logan easily pushed away from the door and walked to the kitchen table, pulling a chair out and sitting down. "That's what you said last night. But I happen to know differently today."

The microwave buzzer sounded and Danella turned, opening the oven door, taking out the container of water and pouring it into the cups. "How do you know differently?"

"Because I want you to spend the afternoon with me. I've been trying to call all morning, but the phone line has been incessantly busy."

Danella chuckled, setting the cups on the table. "Bessie's at it again."

Logan shook his head. "Nope. The last time I called I

had the operator verify it as busy. She said the line was either out of order or the receiver off the hook. That's when I decided to come down and get you. I figured you'd be ready for a change of scenery by the time lunch was over." He reached across the table for the sugar bowl. "Thinking you'd be at Bessie's place, I looked her address up in the phone book and stopped by there first. But instead of finding you, I found an empty house and a note on the door." He stirred his coffee. "So the grandbaby decided to come early, huh?"

Danny nodded, taking a careful sip of the steaming brew.

Logan lolled back in his chair, draping an arm over the top rung. "So as I see it, Danella Jones, there is nothing to keep you from having dinner with me."

"Bessie's invited me to join the family in Wilmington," she said, suddenly panicked by the idea of spending the day with Logan.

"Are you?" Logan asked.

Danny set her cup down, running her finger back and forth through the handle. Keeping her face averted, she shrugged. "If not, I'll probably stay here and work. I've got a lot of things that I really should get done."

Logan shifted in the chair. He reached across the table, took her hand in his, and spoke to her as if to a child. "Today is not the time for you to work, Danny. This is a holiday, a day you spend with people—people whom you care about. It's a family day."

"I can't afford a rush trip home, so I can't be with my family," she explained in a soft voice. "Besides, the plant will be open tomorrow, and I have to work." She lowered her face, not looking at him. "Also, I have that conference in Charlotte this weekend."

"Then why not come and share my home with me."

"Logan," Danny began, "I—"

His grasp tightened, but he didn't hurt her. The

92

touch was warm and reassuring; it was strong. "Come share my family with me, Danny. You'll enjoy it."

Danny's head jerked up, and she stared at him. "*Your* family?"

Logan nodded. "They're up at my condominium, fixing dinner now."

Danny shook her head. "I don't want to intrude on you and your family."

"People only intrude when they aren't wanted or invited. My family and I want you to spend the day with us."

Danny laughed. "I'll bet they do. They don't even know me."

"But I've told them a lot about you, and they're dying to meet you." His voice softened. "They'd like to know you, and they'll like you if you'll just give them the chance."

The silence lengthened until Logan stood. His chair grated against the floor as he pushed it back. Danny watched as he carried his cup to the sink, and she felt her aloneless, her loneliness. She knew that when Logan left she would feel it even more, and she knew that she wouldn't spend one minute on the work that she had brought home.

Reluctantly she agreed with Logan that she needed to get out of the house for a while. She would enjoy being with someone who didn't see her as a usurper; she would enjoy talking to an unbiased soul. She was so lonely, she'd almost developed the habit of talking to herself. She quickly told herself that she wasn't going simply because she wanted to be with Logan Spencer, and she almost believed herself.

Logan turned on the spigot and rinsed out his cup, laying it in the sink. He was aware of Danny's loneliness, and he understood that at this particular point in her life, almost anyone's company would do. While the thought was not pleasant, it didn't deter him. He was determined to make Danella Jones fall in love with him; he resolved that soon her primary reason for wanting to be with him was because he was Logan Spencer. And he would be the only man who could fill her lonely heart. So he was prepared to act cautiously.

"If you're going with me, let me know. I need to call Mom."

His eyes swept over each feature of Danella's face, and it was as if he were touching her—the sleep-tousled hair that gently framed her face, the umber eyes, her mouth, her chin. His gaze dropped to the gentle contours of her breasts, to the creamy swells that were slightly revealed by the scooped neck of her robe.

Her decision made, Danella began to smile. "Give me a few minutes."

Logan nodded. He was glad that Danella was coming with him. She would see him in a different light; she would see his family; she would see him and his family together.

Danny called from her bedroom, "What should I wear?"

"Clothes." Logan chuckled when he heard her impatient snort. "It doesn't really matter," he explained when her face appeared, peeping around the doorframe. "They want to meet you, not look at your clothes."

"But when they meet me, they'll automatically see the clothes I'm wearing," she reminded him. "So what are your mother and sister wearing?"

After Logan told her, Danella resumed scrounging through her closet, looking for the right attire. *This is it,* she thought when she saw the blue-gray pongee dress with the tiny orange flowers. *Plenty dressy without being ostentatious.* Laying her dress on the bed, she darted across the hall into the bathroom, shedding her gown and robe almost before the bolt of the closing door clicked. In record time she brushed her teeth, showered, and dried off.

94

Not bothering with the clutter she left behind, Danny concentrated on dressing, all the time wondering what Logan's family would be like. Excitement and anticipation put color in her cheeks and a smile on her lips. Softly she hummed as she put on her underwear and slipped the shimmering blue-gray material over her head.

Standing in front of the dresser, she deftly applied her makeup and vigorously brushed her hair, grinning as it bounced into place the ends curled under, softly framing her face with auburn beauty. She looped around her neck several gold chains in graduated lengths and put on small gold earrings. Stepping into mid-heeled orange shoes, she turned in front of her mirror, looking at the overall effect.

When she walked into the living room, Logan was sitting in front of the television, watching the pre–football-game commentaries.

"I'm ready."

He immediately stood, his approval glowing in the depth of his blue eyes. "You look lovely, Danny." He smiled. "I think you get more beautiful each time that I see you."

The compliment heightened the glow in Danny's cheeks. "I'll bet you say that to all the girls."

Logan shook his head. "There haven't been that many girls in my life, Danny, and I always tell the truth."

Breaking away from his eye contact, Danny lowered her head, lifted a hand, and began to fidget with her chains. Logan smiled at this woman who could be a power-wielding executive one moment and a soft, vulnerable bundle of femininity the next. He walked to the television and turned it off.

"While you were dressing, I called Mom. She'll be expecting us in about forty-five minutes."

"What's your mother like?" Danella asked as they walked out of the house to the car.

"I'll tell you all I know about her, but nothing I say will prepare you for Willie Sue Spencer." Logan chuckled, sliding under the wheel, keeping up a stream of steady conversation about his family all the way from Blaketon to Wilmington.

It wasn't long until they were driving in front of the condominiums that lined Wrightsville Beach. Nervous now that they were there, Danny didn't hear another word Logan said. She was only vaguely aware of getting out of the car and walking through the main entrance to the elevator. Then they were standing in front of the door. Logan's hand closed over the knob; he twisted and shoved.

"We're here," he shouted as he gently pushed Danella in ahead of himself.

"They're here," Danella heard a feminine voice shriek in return. "Logan and Danny are here."

When the owner of the voice materialized, Danny saw a beautiful woman. "You're Danny." The woman didn't wait for a nod before she caught Danella in a warm embrace; nor did she wait for introductions before she said, "I'm Janet Windham, Logan's sister."

Danella immediately liked Janet, who bubbled with a happiness and excitement that was contagious.

"I've heard so much about you, and I'm glad to meet you at last." Janet stepped back, pushing her hands through her short blond hair. "We knew you had to be something special." She cast twinkling blue eyes on her scowling brother. "Logan has never been so obstinate about our coming to his place for the holidays. And," she added, looking at her husband for support, "he has never brought a girl friend home for us to meet."

Danella smiled, and her face colored softly at the mention of the word girl friend. What had Logan told them? she wondered. "You and Logan look so much alike," she said. "I think I would have known that you were brother and sister without your telling me."

Janet lifted her hand and pressed her nose flat. "All except the nose." She laughed. "Now let me introduce you to my other half."

Ryan Windham, a physician in Charlotte, was a tall, slender man whom Danella soon learned was a devoted husband and father. Much quieter than Janet, he smiled reassuringly, holding out his hand and warmly clasping Danella's.

"Hello, Danella. I'm glad to meet you, and assure you that Janet is not always this talkative. Nor is she always a scatterbrain. But today all of us are likely to be acting rather odd. Having Logan introduce us to a girl friend is rather a novelty. You're a first. So naturally we're not sure just how to react or behave."

Ryan's brown eyes twinkled with life and merriment. Almost as if he knew how nervous Danella must be at meeting Logan's family for the first time, he helped her through the introductions. Having been an outsider once himself, he understood her need for support. He led her to the kitchen. "Mom, here's Logan's little Danny girl."

Willie Sue Spencer, a small, heavy-set woman, turned from the counter where she was spreading marshmallows on sweet potatoes. Looking over the tops of her glasses at Danella, she smiled broadly. Brushing her hands down the sides of the large apron that covered her dress, she rushed to the younger woman, wrapping her arms around her.

"Gracious sakes alive, child, I can't tell you how glad I am to meet you." She bubbled with the same enthusiasm as her daughter. "I always knew Logan would find a good girl. I just didn't know when." She stepped back, adjusting her glasses, studying Danella closely, her blue eyes twinkling with that same warmth and friendliness that both her son and daughter possessed. Willie Sue, always looking on the bright side of things, was a born optimist and took life as it came, meeting it head-on and with a laugh. "I'm glad now that he waited. You're the kind of girl worth waiting for."

"And now, Danella Jones," a deep, resonant voice boomed from the breakfast area, "like the old adage, the best has been saved for last. It's my time to meet you."

Danella spun around and looked into the face of Thomas Spencer, Logan's father. He was a rugged farmer, of medium height but strong. His face was wrinkled from years spent in all types of weather, but each line had character; his expression was pleasant and friendly. His gray eyes were gentle and kind. Walking up to her, he caught her in his arms, giving her a warm, fatherly hug. He gently teased, "I see that my son inherited his dad's good taste in women."

It took Logan's nine-year-old nephew a little longer to get friendly with Danella. Ryan Thomas Windham, called Tommy to avoid confusion, was rather reserved. Never having had to share his uncle with anyone else before, he wasn't sure that he liked his competition. But when he learned that Danella was a whiz at video games, he warmed up.

Danella's Thanksgiving couldn't have been more wonderful. She fell in love with Logan's family immediately, and she never laughed more in her life. They reminded her of her own family, very warm and close, loving and caring. All too soon the beautiful day ended.

"Well, folks," Logan announced from his comfortable position on the sofa as soon as the football game was over, "I guess it's time for Miss Danella and me to be on our way."

"Aw, Uncle Logan," Tommy groaned from the floor, where he and Danny were playing Scrabble. "We haven't finished our game yet, and I'm winning."

"Sorry, sport," Logan teased, leaning over to muss Tommy's hair, "Miss Danella is a working girl, and I need to get her home to bed early."

Tom, lounging in the platform rocker, lazily opened one eye. Lifting his arm, he looked at his watch. "If that's the absolute truth, son, I expect you to be back here in one hour."

"One hour!" Logan yelped. "Give me a break, Dad. "That'll just be enough time—"

"I know," Tom muttered dryly, casting Logan a withering glance. "I'm not senile yet. I'm giving you just enough time to drive Danella home, turn around, and return here. And since this is a weeknight, son, curfew will be earlier than it is on the weekend."

"How late can he stay out, Poppa?" Tommy asked, jumping up and down on the floor. "If it's no later than ten o'clock, Daddy will let me stay up too."

Amidst all the laughing and joking, each one of the family hugged Danella, telling her how glad he or she was that she had come. Willie Sue gave her several jars of homemade preserves and extracted a promise that she would come to Charlotte soon and visit with them.

"Can I go with you to take Danny home, Uncle Logan?" Tommy squealed. "Can I? Huh? Can I? We can play some more interesting games."

Ryan laughed quietly. "Not this time, Tommy. You stay here with us. Uncle Logan and Danny will probably have their own games to play." Ryan looked up at Logan, His lips curved in a teasing smile, his brown eyes dancing with mirth.

"But they won't have much fun without me," Tommy wailed.

"Well," Ryan consoled, barely able to suppress his laughter, "they'll just have to make do, son."

Turning his head, Tommy looked at Logan. "Are you going to come back tonight, Uncle Logan?"

"Yes, he is," Danella returned quickly before Logan could say anything. "I'll send him right back so he can play some more games with you. I'm rather tired of playing games myself." She raised her face to Logan's and whispered, "I don't mind if Tommy comes with us."

Grabbing her hand and leading her out of the condominium, Logan snarled, "Well, I mind. Besides if you want to play games, I have a fantastic one in mind."

"As long as it stays in your mind," Danella quipped in harmony with his family's gentle laughter and the slamming of the door.

As they drove toward Blaketon, Logan and Danella didn't do much talking, but the silence was comfortable. Looking at the passing scenery, Danella smiled as she thought about Logan. She liked him and she enjoyed being with him. At the same time she worried, because she knew just liking Logan wasn't enough. Not only was he demanding more than that from her, she was demanding more from herself. Her biggest concern was in knowing that Logan wasn't the kind of man she should love. Ironically he was the kind of man whom she could love!

At one point Danella turned toward Logan and encountered the honest, open regard of those blue eyes. She saw the question, the desire, that flickered in their depths. She averted her gaze, once again studying the countryside.

Danella wished she could be the kind of woman who enjoyed casual affairs, but she was different. And there was nothing she could do about it; it had nothing to do with Jackie Wesson. Danella Jones wanted more from life than a few nights with first this man and then that one. That was why she had always avoided emotional attachments. She wanted more than a few scattered affairs. She wanted love, a love that brought with it happiness and warmth, a husband, a family.

Yet, when she had seen what love had brought to Jackie, Danny's romantic inclinations had paled, and she had changed the priorities in her life. Because she wouldn't compromise herself with fleeting romances and because she wouldn't chance being hurt from committing herself to a man and then running the risk of being hurt as Jackie had been, she had withdrawn from any kind of intimacy with a man.

Now Logan Spencer dared to dig beneath her cold exterior, exposing and bringing to life her secret desires and wishes. He, the man with no heart, callously invaded her tender one, determined to break fallow ground, and with each step he took, Danny felt that same raw hunger in herself that she had seen reflected in his eyes. She had reason to be wary, she thought. If she wasn't careful, she would give in to this man and his demands. And he in return would give her nothing but a few hours of pleasure to offset a lifetime of heartache and grief.

As she looked into his eyes Danny felt as if her thoughts were written on her face for him to read, and her cheeks warmed with guilt. Logan arched his sandy brows and smiled, wondering what spicy secrets were flitting through her mind. He could see the happiness in her eyes, but he also saw the doubt and uncertainty there, and it concerned him. Danny didn't trust him yet. Shoving his anxiety aside, however, he smiled reassuringly and returned his attention to his driving.

When they turned off the road close to Blaketon Pharmaceuticals, Danny looked at him curiously. "Why are you turning here?"

"I thought we'd go see the grist mill. Do you mind?"

"No, not really.." She squirmed on the seat and stretched. "I've never seen it, and I should take a look so I'll know what to do when I have to decorate it for Christmas.'" Almost before Danny was prepared for it, Logan braked and parked the car in front of the old building.

"Oh, Logan," Danny exclaimed, her eyes scaling the gray, weathered structure. "It's beautiful." With the eye of a person who truly loves antiquity, Danella didn't see a decayed building; rather she saw the mill as it was during its heyday. "It's lovely, and I love it."

Logan, staring at Danella, said softly, "Yeah, I think so too."

Danella heard the sensual undertone, and she dragged her eyes from the mill, leveling them at Logan. Suddenly she felt as if she were on tenterhooks. Too many of his promises haunted her, tormenting her with pleasures foretold. But at the same time, alarm bells clanged unceasingly. She had to keep her distance from this man or he would hurt her terribly.

Letting Logan catch her hand in his, Danny slid across the seat. They got out of the car and walked to the edge of the pond. Neither spoke, both enjoying the symphony of nature, the quiet melody of the forest.

"Howdy, folks," a deep male voice called out. Both Danella and Logan turned and saw a small cart lumber out of the forest across the clearing toward the pond next to which they were standing.

"Hello, Bert," Logan replied, lifting a hand in greeting. "How are things going?"

"Purty good," the man replied, reining the horse to a halt.

"Bert Shaffer," Logan said, "I'd like for you to meet Danella Jones."

"Howdy, ma'am," Bert said, doffing his battered hat. "Shore heard a lot aboutcha, and I'm certainly glad to make yore acquaintance."

Danny walked to the cart and extended her hand, catching Bert's in a firm handshake. "I'm glad to meet you, Bert."

Then Danny backed off, letting the two men talk. Just before Bert drove away, he said, "Tildy and me want ya to come by and have a cup of coffee and a piece of pie or cake with us before ya leave, and I kinda expect Miss Lethia would liketa seeya up at the main house."

When Bert was out of earshot, Logan said, "Bert is caretaker for the grounds at Blake House. I wanted you to meet him and his family so you could learn about the people and they could get to know you."

Danny nodded, bending down to pick up a pine needle. "Does Lethia know that we're here today?"

Logan shook his head. "No, and we don't have to go to the main house if you don't want to." He paused, again regarding her with open honesty. "I didn't drag you out here just to see Lethia, if that's what you're thinking."

Danny smiled, her eyes square on Logan's face. "But you would like for me to."

Logan put both hands in the pockets of his jacket. "I would. Both of you are great ladies, and I would like for you to know each other better. There's no reason for the two of you always to be at loggerheads when you're working toward the same goals."

"Don't you think Lethia would resent our dropping in on her unannounced?"

Logan grinned. "Absolutely not. Country folks are different from city dudes. They have an etiquette of sorts, but theirs is down-home and friendly. They don't mind you dropping in if you're in the neighborhood. They always have a pot of coffee in the makin'."

Danella laughed with Logan, and tears misted her eyes. She couldn't believe how different he seemed from her first impressions of him. It was so out of character . . . She stopped in mid-thought. Or maybe it truly was in character. Maybe she hadn't been able to see his character clearly because of her memories of Jackie. Danny looked up and smiled.

"Maybe I'll become a Blaketonian after all, Logan."

"I'm counting on it," he whispered.

Danny stared at him until she thought she would

drown in the depths of his blue eyes. Finally she dragged her gaze away and focused on the old mill. "It's . . . it's . . ." She cleared her throat. "It's a shame that someone hasn't done something constructive with the mill. It's a shame they let it get so run-down."

Logan smiled, understanding and accepting her retreat. "Bert told me the other day when I was out here with Lethia that it's still functional." His eyes scaled the height and the breadth of the building. "With a little work and ingenuity and a whole lot of capital, it could be transformed." He moved closer to the entrance, running his fingers over the rusted hinges. "Lethia is hoping that eventually Warrington will renovate it, since it was part of Blake Company. It would serve as good publicity and goodwill for the community." He laughed quietly, recalling his discussion with Lethia. "She can really tell you some tales about this place."

As they walked around the exterior of the old building Logan recited the colorful folklore that Lethia had told him, and Danny allowed herself to get caught up in the nostalgia of the past. But at the same time she was definitely in the present, her astute mind working.

They walked inside, ducking through the decaying door, which was coming off its hinges. "If this old mill is part of the Blake tradition, Logan, maybe Warrington should restore it. It could be used for many different things. For instance, it would make a beautiful restaurant, picturesque and nostalgic, and people could enjoy the beauty of the forest all year round rather than just during Christmas."

"Yeah," Logan droned absently, picking up some rusted pieces of equipment off the floor and carefully laying them on the counter that ran around the perimeter of the room. "Lethia also has dreams of seeing it renovated and restored, but she wants a functional grist mill." He wiped his rust-stained hands on his jeans. "Myself, I was thinking of a grist-mill–company-store

104

combination, but"—he looked at her—"it doesn't matter as long as the mill is saved."

Getting excited about the prospect of seeing the old mill restored, Danella said, "I think I'll call Mr. Warrington on Monday and feel him out about this, Logan."

"No need," Logan told her offhandedly. "I'll be going to Atlanta on Monday and I'll mention it." He was so caught up in examining the building, he didn't see Danny's surprised look. "Lethia and I wanted to suggest the reopening of the grist mill, but I'll also tell him about your idea for a restaurant."

Although Danella stood in a stream of sunshine that poured through the broken windows at the top of the building, she shivered. As her eyes scaled the weather-worn gray walls she looked at the abandoned birds' nests and the cobwebs that glistened silver in the sunlight, and she felt the heat of jealousy as it swept through her body. But this time her feelings were slightly altered. She wondered why Logan hadn't told her he was leaving for Atlanta on Monday. Would she always be the outsider, the last one to find out something? she wondered.

"Whose interest will you be representing in Atlanta, Logan?" she asked curtly. "Mine or Lethia's?"

Logan, standing in front of the long worktable, turned and stared at Danella for a long time before he finally spoke. "You still don't trust me, do you, Danella? Have you been wronged so many times during your short life that you have no trust left, or is it just me?" He moved across the floor, not stopping until he stood directly in front of her.

"I'm sorry," she apologized, instantly repentant. "I guess I'm on edge today." She smiled, totally disarming Logan. "I guess I'm just jealous because you and Lethia are insiders and I'm not."

Logan chuckled, because he knew that Danella was skirting the issue at hand. Also, he knew that it was best to let the subject lie for the time being. "Just give yourself time, Danny. Soon people will think that you've been here forever. Why, look at the way Bert took to you. Invited you to coffee and cake right off the bat without even consulting with Tildy. Soon the word will be out and you'll be in."

Danny laughed, pressing close to him when he draped an arm around her shoulder and guided her through the mill, pointing and talking about new ideas for the restaurant as they walked. "But to answer your question and set your fears at rest, I'm not representing any one person's interests at all. I represent all our interests. I think that basically each of us wants the mill saved, and naturally each of us thinks his decision is the best. I'll suggest the alternatives, but Horace will hire a team of experts to study the proposals and make his decision based on their findings." He smiled. "No more of this now. Let's explore the mill and talk about the changes that we want to make."

About an hour later, exhausted after scrambling through the old building, Danny sat down on a soft cushion of pine needles and basked in the warm sunshine that streamed into the mill. Finally tiring of watching Logan climb around, she lay on her back on the thick carpet of dry needles, one hand under her head, the other lying across her stomach. Her eyelids finally grew so heavy that she had to close them.

"Hello, Sleeping Beauty," Logan teased a long time later, easing himself down beside her, awakening her with his soft words and a light kiss. "Time to wake up." Opening her eyes, Danny smiled lazily. Logan stretched his legs and leaned on one elbow, using his free hand to trace the outline of her eyebrows. "I just couldn't resist." Embers ignited behind his eyes, and the flame of desire blazed. "You look rather kissable right now, Ms. Jones."

106

Logan brought his lips tantalizingly close but not close enough. His breath fanned her cheeks, whispering across them. When he saw the raw hunger shimmering in her eyes, he tormented her even more. His gaze, like a magnet, pulled Danny to him. If she had tried, she couldn't have broken away from those eyes, which glowed with passion. Burning brightly in their blue depths were determination and purpose. Danny knew she was about to walk into a furnace of emotion such as she had never experienced before in all her life. And she fully understood exactly what she was doing.

Logan lowered his head in a sweet, tentative kiss, but Danella wanted more; she wanted that aching void fulfilled. Logan, sensing her need, let the kiss deepen, his tongue gently brushing past her lips as it entered the moist richness of her mouth. When Danella's lips and her tongue reciprocated his love touches, Logan groaned in pleasure. His body bent forward and her arms wound around his neck. When he lifted his face, his lips forged a moist path from her mouth to the arched column of her throat, his tongue chasing passion down the side of her neck to that soft, sensitive identation at her shoulder. He buried his face in the scented curve of warm flesh.

"Is Brock still a part of your life, Danny?" he murmured, his breath warm against her skin.

"I'm not sure. Sometimes I think he's a memory from my past," she whispered, thinking of all the excuses Brock had given her for not visiting her and how seldom he called or wrote to her.

"What about your future?" His lips brushed over her face, her eyebrows, the tip of her nose. They traveled across her cheek to her temple; they nipped her outer ear, finding all the small hollows of sensitive delight.

Remembering her dream of long ago, Danny smiled, and her eyes softened. "I want a husband and marriage.

I want at least four children and a home in the country."
Danny forgot about Logan; she forgot about Jackie; the words just spilled from her mouth.

Finally, when she ceased talking, Logan said, "It sounds like you're really a home-and-hearth type."

The thought surprised him. From the way Danella had talked the first night, defining her relationship with Brock, Logan had assumed that she was totally career-oriented.

Danella peered at him. "I guess maybe I will be," she returned, "when I meet the right man."

Logan smiled, his face full of tender indulgence. "A Mr. Right is part of the formula for happiness, isn't it?"

Danella chuckled, nodding her head. "For me he is. I'll only marry for love. And once I'm married, I'm married."

Logan eased over onto his back, lifted his arms and laced his fingers together, locking them behind his head. He stared at the sky a long time before he said, "I've been married, Danny."

Caught by surprise, Danny could only whisper the word. "Married?"

Still without looking at her, he said, "Been divorced for nine years." He waited a moment, then began to talk. "Alma and I married while we were in college. We worked our way through. And we were happy until after we graduated and I got my first job. Then things began to change." He found it strange to discuss his marriage. It was so far back in his past, he had to concentrate to remember what Alma looked like. "When we gave up being college students and really began to live together, we discovered that there was more to a good marriage than making love. We learned that we didn't really love one another; our marriage couldn't stand the test of everyday living: all those little vexations such as bills and work; wanting to keep up with

108

the Joneses when you don't have the money to; fretting when you can't." He paused. "Love is the adhesive that binds two people together in marriage, Danny. Without it, small, pesky irritations become unmanageable. And you soon learn that sex alone is not enough of a healer or a binder. In marriage both partners must love each other completely or it's hell."

Danella sat quietly, thinking about Logan's confession. Eventually, she said, "I agree. That's one of the reasons why I must be sure, Logan, before I make a commitment to any man."

Logan turned his head and looked at her, his lips forming a heart-rending grin. "Are you telling me that you'll only go to bed with a man for love?"

Danny propped herself on her elbow and looked at his face, loving everything about it. "I know it sounds old-fashioned, but that's the way I am, Logan."

Logan didn't move, but the teasing died in his eyes. "What if I told you that I love you, Danny?"

Danella paused for just a second before she replied, "I think it's safe to say that you want me, but I'm not sure that wanting is the same as love."

"You're right, Danny girl, I do want you, and I'd do almost anything to get you. But I promise I love you."

Before Danella was aware of what had happened, Logan had moved, his hands closing about her shoulders. He eased her to the ground beside him. Once again they were cushioned on the bed of brown pine needles, Danella on her back, Logan leaning over her.

"Enough of the past and confessions, Danny. Let's move to our future. Let's think about ourselves. You and me."

Danny stared at him, completely forgetting Jackie, forgetting her own fears and inhibitions, captured by the longing she read in his visage. She studied his eyes as they peered into hers. Lying in the warmth of the sunshine that flooded the quiet old mill, she gazed into that face, which looked so dependable and so sturdy, and she wanted to tell him that she could love him. She could see a little boy who looked just like Logan. That crooked smile, those dancing blue eyes. She could visualize a little girl, her daddy's little darling, a beguiler from the word go, twinkling blue eyes, an enchanting smile.

"Are you a family man, Logan?" she asked.

"Not yet," he chuckled. "But I think I could be easily converted if I should meet the right woman." His voice lowered to that sultry huskiness that Danella loved to hear. "Are you willing to help me out?"

Danella was knocked speechless by the love and tenderness she saw in those sapphire eyes. "I . . . I think I need to think about it," she whispered.

He nodded, holding her close in his arms for a long time before he finally got to his feet, extending a hand to help her. "I guess it's time for us to get going if we're going to have coffee and cake with Bert and Tildy and visit a spell with Lethia."

He pulled her up and she fell across his chest, but she quickly pushed away. Their eyes met, and both were stilled by the undiluted passion that they saw. Logan gently touched her tangled hair. "A pine needle," he said.

Danny took the needle that he handed her, avoiding his gaze. Her breathing was strained, and she was nervous. She couldn't believe that she was allowing this to happen to her. She had learned that heartbreak and despair always follow in the track of passion, cruelly stalking the victim. She was the woman who was determined to approach her relationship with men carefully and cautiously. She was the woman who was going to avoid emotional attachments because they were irrational and degrading. Yet, here she was, running headlong down the same path that Jackie had walked—and with the same man. Danella Jones had learned nothing!

"Danny, spend the night with me."

Ironic, Danella thought, lowering her head and intently studying the pine needle as she pulled it through her fingers. She had always been so careful not to play with fire, and here she was, about to run into a furnace of desire that burned hotter than anything she had ever known. If she went with Logan tonight, there would be no retreating, no turning back. She knew that she would walk through hell if he were to lead her there. It wasn't a matter of yes or no; it was a matter of timing. She dropped the pine needle and looked up at him.

"It's too soon, Logan." The words came out in an agonized whisper. "My feelings are too new. You'll have to give me some more time."

"How about dinner tomorrow night?"

"I'll be working."

"Work," he scoffed, forgetting about her conference. "Surely you don't expect me to believe that."

"The pharmaceutical convention in Charlotte," she murmured. "I'm leaving as soon as I get off work tomorrow afternoon and won't be back until Sunday."

Logan nodded. "And I'm flying to Atlanta first thing Saturday morning." Although he was disappointed, he smiled. "I'll see you when I get back."

Danny nodded. "You'll see me when you get back." She suddenly took a deep gulp of air and smiled. "Now I think it's time for us to leave."

They walked to the car, carefully driving through the woods to Bert's house. Once there, the afternoon passed much more quickly than Danella would have imagined. Matilda, lovingly called Tildy by Bert, was as happy to see them as Bert had been, and true to Logan's word, Tildy had a pot of coffee brewed and a large selection of sweets from which to choose. As they munched on the

111

goodies and drank coffee, they discussed plans for decorating the trees in the famed Christmas Tree Forest. Afterward, Danella, Logan, and Bert returned to the mill so Bert could show them the tour route.

Because the path was narrow, Logan parked the car in front of the mill and he and Danella joined Bert on the cart. As they slowly ambled through the beautiful forest filled with majestic evergreens, Bert described the care that the trees demanded and identified each, pointing them out. Although the forest was planned and cared for, it had a natural beauty that was unexcelled by any that Danella had ever seen.

Then Bert took them to the carriage house and showed them the sleighs that had been specially built for the tours with wheels replacing the runners. Motioning to the path that led to Blake House, Bert suggested they hitch up one and drive to Lethia's. As the horse trotted off, Bert laughingly called out, "Belle probably knows the way better'n you do. If ya want to sight-see, go ahead; she'll just mosey on along."

Pulling Danella into the curve of his body, Logan said, "One couldn't ask for a more romantic setting, could she, Danella Jones?"

"Logan," Danny chided, pushing against him, "Bert is watching us."

"So?" he countered, totally unrepentant, his hands sliding from her shoulders down to the small of her back. "I'll bet he and Tildy take advantage of these buggies."

"If you don't stop," Danny whispered, her eyes darting from Bert, who stood grinning at the horse that ambled leisurely down the pathway, "I'm going to get out and walk."

Logan's lips twitched into that partial grin that caused Danny's heart to do somersaults. "But it's a shame to waste such a beautiful and romantic setting. Mother

112

Nature has done so much for us, and you're not willing to take advantage of her gift."

"Logan!" Danny threatened, a smile surfacing.

"Surely that's not what you want," Logan chided, pulling away from her, touching her only with that endearing grin.

Not even Danella could conceal the clamorous uproar of her emotions. "Perhaps it's not exactly what I want, but for the moment it's what's best for me." Her eyes began to dance, the shining slivers of gray flecked with glints of golden brown, and her lips finally gave way to a warm smile.

"No, sweetheart," Logan said, breathing heavily, his words touching her frayed senses like the cool softness of silk. "I'm what's best for you."

His caress, though verbal, couldn't have been more potent if it had been physical. His eyes, blue like the sky above, promised her untold pleasure and joy. They teased her, slowly outlining the fullness of her lips, tenderly simulating his touch on her, reminding her of his kisses earlier that day.

"But since you haven't yet recognized, my sweet, that I really care about you, that I would never hurt you, I'll just wait." Then he warned in that love-soft voice that caused her heart to flutter erratically, "I fully intend to make love to you." He added audaciously, "I fully intend to marry you, Danella Jones, and I won't give up until I've made you fall in love with me."

His fingers lightened their touch, gently stroking the feverishly hot flesh underneath the soft fabric of her dress. Hot tongues of fire lapped through her body just as he promised, quickly melting any resistance.

"I've never met a woman like you in my entire life, Danella Jones, and I want to make you mine." His voice was soft. His lips brushed against hers, his breath fanning against her cheeks. "I want you to make me yours."

113

She welcomed his sensuous assault, her eyes closing to the burning desire she saw flaring in Logan. She gave in to the ecstasy of the moment. Her hands, as if with a will of their own, slid up his chest, across the muscular plane, around to his back, her fingers kneading into the hard, warm flesh. Then she moaned softly, her lips parting, one hand slipping up to the nape of his neck to pull his lips closer to hers.

With a low snarl of approval his hand cupped the back of her head and his fingers entwined themselves in the silkiness of her hair. Then he was kissing her with a savage and a burning intensity. Gasping in delight, Danella opened her mouth, and his tongue made an immediate and violent invasion, ravaging the musky sweetness.

But the urgency, tempered with love, slowly changed to a gentleness that was immensely satisfying to Danella. His lips lifted and tugged; they nipped and they nibbled. His hands moved from her head, down her shoulders, and elsewhere on her body. When finally his fingers curved around a breast she moaned, and her hand covered his as she writhed with pleasure. No longer caring what was happening, she slipped down on the seat, willingly losing herself in the heat of desire, knowing only that she wanted to be pleased and to please.

She felt his fingertips brush over the burning flesh. Her body trembled with desire, and she clutched him, words of encouragement pouring out of her mouth. Logan's murmurs of love, incoherent though they were, pushed her over the edge of sanity, and his body graphically spoke his needs and desires. She forgot they were in the buggy and headed for the main house; she forgot they were going to see Lethia; she forgot everything but his touch.

Her thought was selfish; she was going to take as much from Logan as she could. She had never tasted desire before, and she was foundering. She was pushing aside her hurtfulness and anguish for all time. She felt his fingers move up her leg under her dress. She gasped when she felt his fingers as they slipped under the elastic of her panties.

"Well, hello! Fancy meeting you here!" Lethia's soft voice carried across the clearing, alerting them to her approach.

Startled, Danny opened her eyes and fought to sit up, her hands clumsily raking through her hair. In no hurry and apparently not embarrassed, Logan straightened, running his hands through his thick, sandy waves. His movement gave Danella time to straighten her dress.

"I think *inopportune* would be the word to use," Logan drawled, his lips twitching into that infernal grin, his blue eyes dancing with amusement.

For the first time since she'd met the woman, Danny noticed that Lethia Blake was really smiling. And she also noticed that the woman had waited until they had surfaced from their embrace before she neared the sleigh. She was dressed in navy blue slacks, a light-blue pullover sweater, and a matching cardigan. She moved quickly toward them.

"I wasn't spying on you," Lethia informed them crisply. "I always walk along this pathway, since it's one that's hardly ever used." She smiled reminiscently. "It was the one that we used to go back and forth to the old mill when I was a child." She looked at both of them. "Have you been to the mill yet?"

After Logan answered Lethia's question, the three of them slowly moved toward Blake House. Walking beside the sleigh rather than riding, Lethia regaled them with stories about the mill. When they reached the house, she invited them in, and they sat in a lovely room that had been converted into a den. As they

115

talked Danella saw a side of the woman that she had never known existed, and she quickly understood why Logan liked and respected Lethia Blake. She was highly intelligent and shrewd, but she also had the potential for being friendly and gracious.

Just before night fell, Logan stood. "I guess we'd better get going. We've got to return Belle and the sleigh to the carriage house."

"I'm glad you came," Lethia said, walking them to the door. "By the way, Danella, I . . . I thought about what you said the other day, and against my better judgment, I talked with Curtis and Bowen." She hesitated. "They've agreed to stay for six more months to see how you manage Blaketon Pharmaceuticals." She almost chuckled at Danella's shocked expression. "When the other transferees see that these two are going to give Warrington a chance, I think they'll reconsider also."

"Thank you," a flabbergasted Danella mumbled. She had never expected this.

"Don't thank me," Lethia returned crisply. "I did it for Blaketon Pharmaceuticals. I did it because you're convinced they're good for the company." She added, "I'm not sure about them yet."

And thank you again! Danella seethed silently, looking at Logan in time to see him squelch the grin that threatened to play across his lips.

"Have you decided what you're going to do with the forest this year?" Lethia asked.

"I'm going to have clear lights strung in the trees so we can create a wintry scene, an icicles-and-snow effect. Using the new equipment and sound system I've requisitioned, we'll play Christmas songs and use soft colored lights. College students will be happy to run the tours for us, and choral groups from different organizations will donate their time for the caroling at the old

116

mill. Bert said he has several men doing minor repairs on the chapel to get it ready for services."

Lethia smiled. "Neither of you has ever seen the chapel, have you?" Both of them shook their heads, but Lethia wasn't looking. She was lost in nostalgia, her voice tender and sweet, evincing none of the bitterness and harshness to which Danella was accustomed. "It's beautiful. The sleigh bells tinkling, the soft Christmas music, the beautiful trees. Services in the chapel. Just you wait and see." She smiled again, and this time the smile actually reached her eyes, twinkling in their depths. "I've always thought it would be an ideal setting for a wedding."

Logan looked at Danella and grinned, watching her face as it turned a deep crimson.

CHAPTER FIVE

Thanksgiving Day seemed to be the turning point in Danella's personal life as well as her career in Blaketon. The next morning Curtis and Bowen announced their intention of staying with the company for six months on a trial basis, and the weekend conference in Charlotte was successful for Blaketon Pharmaceuticals contractwise. While Danny and Lethia had not become friends, they began to work well together. Each of them had a healthy respect for the other. Most important of all, Logan called Danny every day that he was gone, and on Wednesday—the day of the interview with Jane Harris—he sent her a dozen pink roses.

But that wasn't all. Not forgetting his promise to give Danella support, he arrived at Blaketon Pharmaceuticals just before the interview—the first time that Danny had seen him in six days. If she lived to be one hundred, Danny thought, she would never forget the moment when the door to her office opened, the moment when she looked up and saw Logan. She was totally unprepared for the shock that jolted through her. Never had passion mixed with desire shot such acute longing through her limbs. Her legs were so weak, she thought they would buckle under her own weight; her stomach was filled with hundreds of fluttering butterflies; her head was giddy and light. Inside she was nothing but a mass of jittery nerves.

His grin was just as endearing as ever, his physique just as virile, but the expression in his blue eyes was brooding and somber as they raked over her blue suit and white blouse. "Miss me?" he asked. That wasn't really the question at all, and both of them knew it. He was asking, *Do you still want me?*

Danny was out from behind her desk, moving toward him as quickly and surely as he was moving toward her. She nodded slowly, answering both the spoken and the unspoken words. "I missed you. I thought the week would never end."

And when his lips touched hers, words were forgotten as their bodies rediscovered the joy of each other. Giving in to the emotion that racked his body and shook his soul, he moaned deeply, his arms slipping around her, hugging her softness to his hard frame.

His lips opened, and the kiss deepened as he searched for her soul. Danny, just as hungry, rose up on her toes, pressing herself against him, her hands sliding beneath his navy blue suit coat and around him. She felt his intake of breath as her fingers touched his back, exploring the hard muscle there.

All inhibitions and fears were cast aside; Jackie Wesson's warnings were totally eradicated from her memory. Danella Jones was on her way to falling in love with Logan Spencer. Danella Jones was discovering a new and exciting Logan Spencer.

"Dear Lord, Danny," Logan murmured when he finally broke the kiss, his words ragged, his breathing uneven, "I don't ever want to be separated from you again. Being away from you is hell."

119

But even as he muttered the words, both of them knew he had wedged the interview in between two important meetings. And as soon as he finished there, he would be flying to Raleigh. But they had each other right now. They knew they had to make the most of the moment. They must be thankful that they had this time together rather than bemoan their coming separation.

"I wish I didn't have to leave you so soon," he murmured.

"It can't be helped," Danny consoled him. "Besides, I'm just glad to have you here, even if it's for only half a day."

"That's just it, my sweet. I'm a greedy man, and I'm finding that a half a day, a few minutes here and there, are not enough for me." He moved slightly, the pressure of his body changing, alerting Danny to the needs that surged through his body. "It's not long enough for me to tell you or to show you what you mean to me, darling."

Danny made no reply; instead she lowered her head and tucked her face against his chest. At the moment she felt too vulnerable, too susceptible, to utter a word, to let him see how deep her attraction to him was.

But even now Jackie's memory rudely intruded into Danella's thoughts. She tried to block it out but couldn't. All at once she was afraid—afraid of this man who was coming to mean so much to her; afraid that if she gave in to him, he would one day discard her, leaving her brokenhearted, trying to pick up the pieces of her life.

The ominous warning flashed through Danella's mind, but she forced it aside. After all, she had spent weeks in the presence of this man, and she knew him. And if that had not been enough to convince her of his sincere intentions, Thanksgiving Day had. She thought of that as her test case. She had really seen Logan Spencer—the man, the son, the brother—as he really was. She

120

had seen him with his family; she had seen him with Bert. This Logan was the man whom she could love. He was nothing like the Logan Spencer that Jackie Wesson had told her of.

"Tell me this isn't all one-sided," Logan chided softly, pulling away slightly, looking down at her, wondering what she was thinking. "Tell me that you're feeling the same way."

"I'm glad that you were able to come for the interview, and I'm glad for any time that we get to spend together," she confessed, adding on a much softer note, "but . . . but I want more too." Still, she didn't move her head to look up at him; rather, she ran her finger up and down the silk material of his shirt. Frightened of the intimacy, frightened of the way their relationship was deepening, Danny bolted and ran. "How was Atlanta?"

Logan, understanding her fears, chuckled. "I'm not sure, but even if I were, I wouldn't want to talk about it now. I just want to feel, Danny, to feel you and to feel what you're doing to me." He chuckled. "Horace accused me of having my mind on other things. He said he had never seen me so distracted before." The soft chuckle burgeoned into unrestrained laughter. "And he was so right. Only my body was there, Danny girl. My spirit was with you wherever you were." Now Logan's fingers gently tapped her chin, and he lifted her face. "He asked me if I was in love."

"Are you?" Danella asked, barely able to get the words out.

"I think I am." He smiled. "What about you?"

"I don't know. I—I think I could be."

The interview with Jane had gone well; Logan had seen to that. Danella could remember answering all the questions, but it was as if she were floating, as if she were in a beautiful world just beyond reality. After the interview she, Logan, and Jane had lunched together, which allowed for no personal discussions between the two of them. After lunch they returned to Blaketon Pharmaceuticals and said good-bye to Jane, but Logan and Danella sat in his car a little longer, savoring their last few minutes together.

"Now, Mr. Spencer," Danella said softly, "tell me about your trip to Atlanta. What did Horace have to say?"

Logan shook his head, wearily rubbing his fingers over the bridge of his nose. "We just went over two more jobs that I'm doing for him, and I briefed him about the progress of publicity on Blaketon Pharmaceuticals. I turned in all the suggestions that had been made about restoring and possibly converting the mill, and he took it, glanced through it, and threw it to the side of his desk."

"He . . . he didn't seem interested in it?" Danny questioned, feeling disappointed.

"He wasn't interested or uninterested. He said he would look it over and give it some thought. And you know Horace: He's a man of his word. He'll do just that."

"In his own good time," Danny conceded.

Logan smiled, reaching across the seat to catch both her hands in his. Gently he squeezed. "Let's not discuss work right now, darling. I've got so little time to spend with you. I just want it to be the two of us that fills my memory, not work, and certainly not Horace Warrington."

If Logan seemed reticent to discuss the particulars of his visit with Warrington, Danny was too excited to notice it, and she gladly went along with any suggestion he made. They sat in the car and talked until it was time for Logan to go. He promised her that he would be back Friday so he could help with the decorating of Christmas Tree Forest.

And he had come back. Bright and early Friday morning, dressed in a flannel shirt, jeans, heavy jacket, and work boots, he picked Danny up and drove her out to the grist mill. They worked all day, but there was still more to be done. Danny walked out of the mill, heading for Logan's car. She lifted her face and smiled, glad the day was sunny and warm and that they had made inroads into the decorating of the forest. Bert and Logan had promised that they would be finished by the next evening. It would be ready in plenty of time for the official opening Sunday evening.

She lifted her hands and ran them through her hair. Then she lazily leaned against the car, crossing her legs and folding her arms over her chest. She heard the mill door squeak as it announced another departure. Looking up, Danella watched Lethia step out. Dressed casually in slacks and a shirt, she looked as if she had just left her house. Not a strand of her hair was out of place, but Danny knew for a fact that the woman had worked as hard as the rest of them.

Lethia walked up to Danella, a look of uncertainty in her eyes. "Would you like to join me for dinner tonight? In fact," she added, "you could just spend the night at the house so you won't have much of a drive tomorrow when you return."

"Thanks," Logan answered for Danny as he rounded the corner of the building with Bert, "but not tonight." He laid the wiring in the bed of Bert's truck and slapped his hands against his jeans. "I've already made plans to take Danny out to eat in Wilmington. Got the reservations and everything." Bert and Lethia exchanged knowing grins, and Danny colored with pleasure as Logan walked up to her and put his arm around her shoulders. "Danella's been working too hard. She needs some rest, relaxation, and special attention," he said, as his fingers squeezed into the soft flesh of her upper arm.

"Where are we going?" Danny asked later in Logan's car as they began to drive away.

"I thought we'd eat at the Treasure Chest," he told her. "Great seafood restaurant on the beach."

Momentarily apprehension enshrouded Danella as she envisioned the bright neon lights and the picture of the large, bearded pirate carrying the chest. The restaurant, she realized was located in Logan's condominium building.

"Okay?"

"Uh-huh," she answered, quickly pushing her doubts aside. "I'll need to go by the house and change out of these jeans."

When they arrived at Danny's house, she hurried into the bedroom not realizing that Logan was following. She lifted her underwear out of its drawer and began to unbutton her shirt when she turned around to find him leaning nonchalantly against the doorframe.

He couldn't hear her sharp intake of breath, but he could see her hand stop in mid-motion; he could see her body tense. "Sorry," he said, smiling a little sheepishly. "I guess I should have said something." She walked to the closet and took out a plaid skirt and matched it with a solid sweater. "This okay?"

"Fine." He wasn't even looking at the outfit; he was staring at Danella.

"I'm serious, Logan," she reprimanded as she pulled out a pair of matching shoes.

"I am too." He grinned, but his eyes did casually sweep over the clothes she held, and he added, "The colors are beautiful."

Laying her outfit on the bed and picking up her underwear, she turned and started to walk toward the bathroom. As she passed him he moved so that her body rubbed against his. "Danny, you know it's going to happen sooner or later."

Danny didn't reply; she merely continued into the bathroom. Standing in the doorway, she said, "Nothing is inevitable, Logan. Each of us controls his or her own destiny."

"Do we, now, Danny girl?" The mockery was gentle and sweet, bringing a rush of color and heat to Danny's cheeks. "I hope those words taste as good when you eat them."

As Danny closed the door behind her, Logan chuckled, moving out of the doorway into the living room. Sitting down on the sofa, he picked up a magazine and thumbed through it while he waited. About twenty minutes later she stepped into the room.

"How do I look?"

He slowly rose to his feet, his gaze sweeping up and down her slender frame several times. "Very good, Danella Jones. Almost good enough to eat."

She dropped the strap of her purse over her shoulder, draped her jacket over her arm, and hooked the other hand around Logan's arm. "But I'm not on the menu tonight," she said, her eyes beguiling.

"A lady with spirit," he taunted, his own eyes gleaming in appreciation.

"A lady with an appetite," she quipped.

"Let's hope that it's a big one, then, lady, because I warn you, I'm definitely on the menu."

His gentle laughter caressed Danny, sending shivers of delight down her spine, but she wasn't daunted. If anything, she was more exhilarated. Glowing with happiness, she accompanied Logan to the car, and her excitement continued to grow as they whiled away the miles from Blaketon to Wilmington. When they walked through the large lobby of the Buccaneer Royal Resorts, Danny's smile and radiance attracted the glances of many passersby, filling Logan with pride.

"Do you like living in a condominium?" she asked as they rode up in the elevator.

"Fits my life-style to a *T*," he told her, guiding her down the corridor to his door. "I don't have to worry about maintenance or about leaving."

He unlocked the door and strode across the living room, turning on the lamps at the end of the sofa. "Want a drink?" he asked, moving toward the bar.

Danny nodded, telling him what she wanted. While he poured it, she walked around, looking at the room more closely than she had on Thanksgiving. That day she had been more interested in the people she would meet than the place. She had been fascinated by his interaction with his family. Now she could leisurely assess the man in his environment.

Watching Danny as she looked around the room Logan said, "What do you think?" When she turned an inquiring face toward him, a grin flashed across his hard, sensual lips. "We had so many other things on our mind Thanksgiving, we didn't discuss the house too much." He walked up behind her, handing her a glass of orange juice and vodka. "Do you really like it?"

"It looks like you," she replied. "Bold and aggressive. Almost intimidating."

"Do I intimidate you?" He lifted his glass to his lips, sipping the drink.

"At first you did," she answered honestly, widening the distance between them, walking to the large window, and looking at the moon-streaked ocean below.

"I don't want to intimidate you," he softly informed her, never moving, yet closing the gap between them. "I want to love you." He paused. "I want to make love to you. . . . In every conceivable way I want to show you how much you mean to me."

Danny had known that this would happen when she accepted his invitation to dinner. Even as she had denied his allegation, she had known that this was inevitable. But thinking it, dreaming about it, fantasizing about it, was different. Now that Logan had verbalized his intentions, now that she was out of her territory and in his, Danny was apprehensive. This was too much for her, too soon. She had to escape the seductive web that Logan was weaving about her. But she found that she could do nothing; she was a victim of her own emotions. She heard him set his glass down on the bar and she turned.

"Be right back," he told her. "I'm going to take a shower."

Danny watched as Logan lazily pulled his shirt from the waistband of his jeans and began to unbutton it. She couldn't take her eyes off the copper-colored chest that was revealed.

"Make yourself at home," he directed, moving in the direction of the bedroom.

He was gone for a few minutes, and Danny heard drawers open and close. She heard the spray of the shower. Softly she heard Logan call from the bedroom door, "You're welcome to wash my back if you want, Danny girl." Intimately his voice lowered. "I'd do anything to persuade you."

Danny didn't move from the window, but she spun around, her eyes riveted on Logan's body. Only his midsection was covered with a towel. He had done that on purpose, she knew. He was trying to push her over the brink. And he was doing it without touching her, without saying anything. He was tantalizing her senses and whetting her desires, making her wonder what he looked like totally naked.

Averting her eyes from the maddening stark white strip of terry cloth, Danny swallowed the passion that nearly choked her. "Not . . . not tonight."

She heard him chuckle as he ducked behind the closing door. Then the quietness of the room began to close in on her; Logan's presence was everywhere, touching her, persuading her. Why had she allowed herself to be manipulated into coming to his condo? Why had she allowed herself to fall in love with him? Hadn't she learned anything from Jackie's ordeal?

"Need a refill on your drink?" Logan's word startled Danny, and she almost jumped.

She hadn't heard him enter. She shook her head and mumbled, "No—no, thank you."

He devastated Danny with his presence, with his casual masculine aura. He was dangerously sensual, and he had never looked more attractive. His wash-worn jeans clung to his legs. His gray and blue shirt complemented the color of his eyes. His sandy brown hair, still damp, was neatly combed away from his face. He looked innocent and warm and unassuming . . . but Danny knew differently. The hunter was closing in on his prey. The warmth and tenderness in the blue eyes didn't disguise his intent; the indolent stance of his body didn't hide his purpose. Would she be able to resist him? she wondered

And if you're not careful, Danella Jones, a voice nagged, *you could be just another trophy on the wall of his heart. Just a trophy for him. A broken heart for you.*

"Is it all right if we eat up here?"

Danny heard Logan ask the question, but it was as if she were in a great vacuum. She could hear, but she couldn't speak. Finally she nodded. Not moving, she watched Logan lift the phone and order their dinner. He refilled her glass and guided her to the sofa, but he didn't sit beside her. Instead he sat across the room in the large occasional chair. He talked and she listened. She laughed with him. She drank with him. She ate with him.

Lulled into a false sense of security by the distance they sat apart from each other, Danella let him ease the last barrier down. She wasn't really sure when it had dropped. Her hunger sated, she kicked off her shoes and curled up in the corner of the sofa, sipping a glass of wine and listening to the deep softness of Logan's voice. She relaxed and allowed herself to be enveloped by his warmth and charm. She allowed herself to forget all about Jackie Wesson. Logan dominated her entire consciousness. He was her senses. She could smell him, see him, hear him. But she wanted more. She wanted to touch him and she wanted to taste him. She was starved for him.

"How about another glass of wine?"

Her reverie shattered, Danella lifted her face, looking at Logan, shaking her head. Then Logan moved and he was sitting on the sofa beside her. When he reached for her hands, she pulled them away.

"Don't"—she cleared her throat—"please don't." She lifted her gray eyes to his inquiring blue ones.

"Stay with me tonight, Danny. Let me show you what love can be like. Love me."

Averting her gaze from his, Danny leaned forward, her fingers curling around the wine goblet, and she lifted the almost empty glass to her mouth.

"Please, Danny."

"No."

She set her empty glass on the coffee table and stood, walking to the window and staring at the silvery ocean below. She had known better than to come. Foolishly she had swept aside Jackie's warnings, and now she was losing her heart, losing it to a man who looked on this entire escapade as a game and her as the prize. She was losing to a man who didn't know the meaning of commitment or responsibility, a man who left broken hearts strung behind him—a man she desired above all others.

Danny's refusal, however, didn't convince Logan. He

knew she was lying. His awareness of her was uncanny. He could tell what she was thinking just by looking at those expressive eyes or the tilt of her head. And he knew that although her fears and anxieties had surfaced and she was fighting with her conscience, she would be staying.

Logan moved across the carpet silently, quickly. "Danny, I'm not going to touch you. I want to but I'm not going to." She heard his voice soften. "I guess I want to know that you desire me as much as I desire you, so you'll have to make the next move. Tell me what you want me to do."

The words pushed everything from Danny's mind but her longings and her cravings. She spun around, facing him. If there were regrets and recriminations, she would save them for later. Tonight she would give in to the dictates of her body. Swaying toward him, closing her eyes, she lifted her face, waiting for his touch. His hands tentatively clasped her shoulders, and he drew her into his embrace in the gentlest and sweetest movement that Danella could have imagined.

He held her for the longest time, his cheek resting on the top of her head, her cheek cradled against his chest. Soothing. Reassuring. She could hear the heavy pounding of his heart; she could hear his breathing; she could feel the tensed muscles; she could sense the desire that whipped through his body, barely held under control. Finally his hands cupped her chin and her neck; his thumbs gently stroked the sensitive fullness of her lips.

"It was destined," he whispered, his lips brushing against hers. "Fate meant us to be together. That's why you were literally swept into my arms, Danny girl." His lips, in tender assault but with loving patience, pressed against hers.

She trembled from the onslaught of emotion that

raged through her body. "Yes," she murmured, tears misting in her eyes as she wondered at the cruelty of fate. Then she wondered no more; she thought no more. She accepted the inevitable. Giving in to his loving persuasion and to the tidal wave of desire, her resolve crumbled into submission.

His fingers stroked her stomach, and she felt her sweater sweeping up over her head. She felt her breasts released from the confines of their filmy halter. Her eyes opened wide and she stared into Logan's eyes. His face lowered and his lips nibbled and bit along the satiny swell until he reached the rosy crest. With adoring strokes his tongue swirled slowly around the inflamed peak until finally his mouth closed around it, sucking with infinite tenderness.

Danny groaned softly, her stomach churning with an insatiable hunger. She moved instinctively against his hard frame, and her hands locked behind his head, drawing him closer, defying him to leave her. Frantically she held on, afraid she'd fall if she didn't. Her legs felt like jelly, and evocative splinters pricked her all over. She twisted her shoulders, shifting her breasts, softly sighing, acutely aware of her growing, aching hunger.

When Logan lifted his head, gathered her into his arms, and carried her to the bedroom, she offered no argument. She didn't know what the future held for them, but she knew that she wanted him, wanted the pleasure he promised, the fulfillment he held for her. She lay on the bed and, through passion-glazed eyes, watched him quickly shed his clothes. In the dim light that streamed in from the living room, she watched his powerful body as he moved toward her. She saw him standing beside the bed.

"You're beautiful," she murmured, lifting her hand, her fingers touching the downy growth below his navel.

As her fingers slid down the path of hair she felt his sharp intake of breath; she felt his stomach contract and tighten. Her eyes ran upward along his body and met his, and she smiled. She ran her tongue over her fevered lips, glazing them with shimmering desire, and she felt Logan tremble. Her hand lowered, and her fingers gently curved around his warm flesh. She marveled in her prowess as a woman when she felt the convulsive tremors that racked him.

"How much of this do you think I can stand?" he whispered unevenly.

He sat down on the bed beside her, and she lifted her shoulders, easing the waist of her skirt over her hips, wiggling out of it and dropping it over the edge of the bed. Then Logan took over the task of undressing her. His fingers hooked around the elastic band of her panties, and he lowered himself onto the bed. His lips began to whisper down her neck, over her breasts and the flatness of her stomach. His hands pushed the fluff of lace down her legs, tracing excruciating pleasure trails along her thighs, her calves, and her ankles as he kissed the taut, tremulous plane of her stomach.

"See, Danny girl," he rasped, gazing at her naked body, which glowed in the muted light. "I'm not going to hurt you. I'm just going to love you."

His voice dropped to a faint whisper as his lips, moist and warm, trailed the line of her collarbone, thrilling her with their passionate searching. His hands explored her body leisurely, delighting her with their wondrous discoveries, and his pleasure heightened with her whimpers of joy.

His fingers traced paths of fire up her inner thighs, treading lightly over the crown of femininity, causing her body to convulse with raw desire as he promised her more. Her blood coursed through her veins and pounded in her head; her pulse beat frenetically. Even if she could have, she wouldn't have resisted his touch.

Never had she ridden so high on sensuous pleasure before. Never had she imagined such exquisite torment. Her body of it's own volition moved with him and for him, perfectly in tune with his every command and desire. She had never imagined that loving could be wild and torrential and at the same time flowing and smooth. She didn't understand how such physical expressions could bring a man and a woman together in such close spiritual bonds, a consummate union of body and soul.

Her hands grasped the hair at the nape of his neck, and she guided his face up to hers. Her lips, long denied this delicacy, captured his, and she pulled his warm sweat-moistened body over hers. She was ready for the natural culmination of their lovemaking.

His knee gently insinuated itself between her thighs, making way for him. His hands explored, his fingers sending exquisite shimmers of pleasure through her body as he stroked her. She was ready, he knew. She was moist and warm; she was gently rotating her hips. She wanted him as urgently as he wanted her.

"Logan," she cried, desire pulsating and throbbing in her lower body, "please—please love me."

Her heartfelt cry touched Logan's very soul. "I will, darling. I will."

His uppermost thought wasn't for himself. Rather, he wanted to give her complete pleasure. He wanted to convince her of his love, in turn asking for hers. Although desire raged through him, he exerted his control. Skillfully he would tutor her in the ways of love, guiding her to that high pinnacle. He would make her love him as he loved her. He would show her the difference between sexual attraction and love.

"Danny girl," he said thickly, his hand stroking her cheek with reverential tenderness, "you're so sweet." He acquainted her with the weight of his body, touch-

133

ing hers most intimately, gently alerting her to his pulsating need. His lips pressed against hers, tenderly parting them wider and wider in an open kiss.

At the same time that his tongue filled her mouth, Danella felt his hardness, and she stiffened. Momentarily she tensed, her face twisting from his, a small gasp hissing through her lips. Then she gripped his shoulders tightly.

Surprised, Logan stopped and waited. He dared not believe! Now he must be even more careful! So much more tender. He stroked her and whispered to her, his lips soft and soothing as they reassured her. When he felt her relax, when she wrapped her arms around him, when her mouth sought his, Logan sighed, letting the joy of his astonishment filter through his body.

His hands cupped her firm buttocks, and he held her close. *Truly,* he thought, *this will be a night of love.* With loving patience, in absolutely no hurry, he guided her through the nuances of love. He encouraged her; he praised her, his lips finally catching hers again in a blazing hot kiss. When the moment came, his tongue slipped into the moistness of her mouth, and his masculinity moved deeper and deeper into the warm haven of her intimacy, stroking, rekindling the flame of desire.

As the fire of their love burned brighter Danella began to respond naturally. Her lips tugged gently, sipping his sweetness, and her tongue sought entrance into the depth of his mouth. Instinctively her body gave love for love received. With no guidance from him, her hands began to travel his body, stroking and caressing, exploring every inch of him.

Her hips swayed with his motion, her anticipation mounting with his. They clung together, moving with and for each other. Their breathing became more ragged and labored; their kisses fuller. Higher and higher they climbed until they felt as if they'd shattered into a million tiny pieces. But Logan didn't abandon her. Gently he rolled onto his side, brushing his hands up and down her back from her shoulders to her buttocks, and his lips kissed the thin sheen of perspiration from her face. He whispered his thanks over and over again.

Then they lay in sublime peace, lingering in love's afterglow, hardly moving, barely breathing, not daring to break the beauty of the moment that bound them together. Danella's shudders ceased, her trembling quieted, and she lay in the protective circle of his arms, her face hidden in the brown hair that covered his chest. They breathed deeply, filling their lungs with the scent of each other, slowly letting their heartbeats return to normal.

A long time afterward Logan spoke. "Why didn't you tell me?"

"There was no reason to," she quietly informed him, contentment giving a lethargic dreaminess to her voice. She was too happy to think beyond this very moment, this time that belonged unequivocally to them.

Cuddling together, they softly shared their lives—the joys, the heartaches, the goals, and the dreams. It wasn't long, however, before Danella fell into a deep slumber. Logan, however, didn't go to sleep as quickly. Instead he wrapped his arms around Danella and held her close. Finally, just before daybreak, he dozed off, not awakening until he heard the rude clanging of the alarm. Disengaging his arms and legs from Danella, he lifted an arm, reached out, and turned it off. Then he rolled over, again pulling her close.

"This feels so good," he murmured, his mouth brushing against her ears.

"What?" Danella asked drowsily, her voice soft and full of joy. "Snuggling back under the covers or me?"

"You," he replied with the same softness. "The joy of waking up to find you in my bed. The pleasure I get from holding you in my arms."

As he spoke his hands gently swept from her back to her buttocks, his fingers exploring their round firmness, pressing her femininity against his hard body. But there was no urgency in his touch this morning. Instead it was slow and leisurely. Knowledgeable of every curve and plane on her body, he now reassured himself that she was his.

"When are we going back to the mill?" Danella asked in a faraway voice that told Logan she didn't really care if they ever did. At the moment she, too, was right where she wanted to be.

Groaning, Logan pulled himself up in bed and raked his hands through his sleep-tousled hair. "Oh, Lord, Danny! I can't think of anything more distasteful this morning than giving up a bedful of pleasures with a beautiful, sexy woman to go unload poinsettias and holly and string Christmas-tree lights."

Danny languorously stretched her willowy body, not quite surfacing from the cover, the sheet riding low on her breasts. She fluffed the pillows behind herself and, using her elbows, crawled into a propped-up position.

"If you're not going to do anything more constructive" —her eyes twinkled mischief—"why don't you brew us some coffee. Maybe some toast and jelly to go with it."

Drawing a face and feigning indignation, Logan howled, "Me? Why me? You're the woman."

Danella touched his bare chest with the tip of her finger. "But you're the host, and I'm your guest. Besides, you told Lethia and Bert that you were going to give me special attention."

Upon hearing those words, Logan growled. "What do you think I've been doing, woman?"

Laughing happily, they donned a pair of Logan's pajamas between them: He wore the bottoms, she the top. Teasing each other, they went into the kitchen and brewed a pot of coffee and made some toast. After they ate, they cleaned up the clutter and went back to the bedroom to shower and dress. While she waited for Logan to shave, Danella wandered through the house, picking up her clothes, but she didn't immediately put them on. Rather, she sat on the side of the bed and leaned back against the pillows that she had propped against the headboard, closing her eyes and reminiscing on the beauty of their night together and the pleasure they had given to one another.

"Another invitation?" Logan asked softly, standing by the bed, looking down at her.

Danella's heavy eyelids slowly lifted, and she gazed at him, the stardust of passion softly blowing in her eyes. He sat down beside her and his fingertips began to trace her features lightly. They feathered over her eyebrows and brushed under one of her eyes, across the bridge of her nose, and under the other eye. The fingertip touched her ear, outlining it in detail.

Danella shuddered as his hand moved from her ear to her throat, sliding down the tenuous plane, again touching and remembering. Just like the fairy-tale prince, his touch created magic with her emotions, awakening them, sensitizing them as they had never been before.

Logan stretched out beside her, letting the towel fall from his body. He propped himself up on one elbow without interrupting his delightful exploration of Danella's body. He pushed the pajama top aside, and his fingers traced back and forth across her collarbone. His hand moved deeper, and he stroked the fullness of a breast that was visible in the deep V of the neckline. He smiled when Danella gave herself to his caresses, and he rejoiced when she moved her body in rhythm to the erotic strokes.

"Logan," Danella gasped, sucking in deep gulps of air. "I love you. I need you."

As she mouthed the words his tongue began to trace

the hardening tip of her breast through the pajama top. Then he began to chart a leisurely course to her mouth. Once there, his lips lightly rubbed over hers in a tantalizing, tormenting gesture. "And I love you," he whispered, his warm breath blowing across her cheeks.

Tired of the torment, no matter how exquisite or enjoyable, Danny's hand cupped the back of his head, and she pressed his face against her. His mouth hardened as his kiss deepened, and she willingly opened her mouth to his gentle invasion. His tongue flicked inside, stroking and exploring the velvety recesses. Then his mouth left hers, retracing its way, leaving behind stinging little nips of pleasure as he moved downward.

When his face rested against her waist, his journey stopped, and he rested his cheek against the soft material of his pajama top. He wrapped his arms around her and he gripped her tightly, as if he never wanted to let her go. Her giving herself to him was the most precious gift he had ever received in his life, and he wanted to hold it and treasure it. He never wanted to betray her love and her trust.

"I've never known love before," Danny whispered, overflowing with her joy, basking in the aftermath of love beautifully demonstrated through physical expression. "I love you, Logan. I love you with all my heart."

She smiled tenderly, touching his mop of sandy hair with her fingers. She entwined her fingers through the locks, luxuriating in her newly acquired freedom from doubt and uncertainty. Once and for all time Jackie's nightmares were totally obliterated, and she trusted Logan. She believed him. She remembered his sweetest promise: *I won't hurt you if you get close to me*.

"Say something," she teased. "Let me know what you're thinking. Surely this isn't all one-sided." Her words were soft, flavored with love, spiced with dreams for a wonderful future.

Logan roused himself from his dreamworld and chuckled. "No, Danella Jones, this isn't all one-sided." He lifted a hand, sliding his index finger down the bridge of her nose. "I . . . love . . . you." His declaration, though faintly spoke, was overflowing with truth. Danny couldn't doubt the intensity of his feeling for her. Yet, she, too, was attuned to Logan's body and his psyche. She divined that something was wrong.

"What is it, darling?"

Logan didn't immediately answer. He pulled one arm from around her and began to play with the snap on the pajama top. Why was he hesitating? she wondered. What was the matter? Had she disappointed him? Was he disappointed in her lack of experience?

"You're the first woman I've ever loved, Danny." He spoke quietly and painfully. "I . . ." He paused. ". . . I cared for Alma, my wife, but I never really loved her."

Danella could sense a hurt; she could feel the pain that emanated from him, but she couldn't understand his hesitation. She began to feel the cold hand of apprehension as it touched her heart. Had she been a fool to trust him, to fall in love with him?

"I'm afraid of losing you." He lifted his face and gazed into hers. "And I don't think I can stand that."

Danella's lips suddenly curved into a large smile, and she laughed aloud. Her expression was warm and brilliant, like sunshine finally breaking through thick black rain clouds. All her worry and anxiety was for nothing. "You're not going to lose me, darling. I'm yours for life." Her eyes glimmered, gorgeous glints of silver shooting through the golden-brown depths. "I guess you know what that means, don't you?" Without waiting for him to answer, she said, "I want to marry you, and the sooner the better." Her umber eyes glowed as she teased, "I could be pregnant, you know."

Logan's eyes assumed a misty softness that Danella

139

had never witnessed before, and when he spoke, his voice was the sweetest that Danny had ever heard. "I should have asked, darling. It was wrong of me to assume. Ordinarily I don't." He lifted a hand and gently brushed the hair from her face. "I promised you that I wouldn't hurt you, yet I made love to you without making sure that you were protected. I just didn't think."

"It's not all your fault," Danny gently pointed out. "I should have said something." Her eyes twinkled. "I may be inexperienced, but I'm not naive." She reached up, cupping his face in both hands. "I was also too caught up in our passion, darling, to give protection a thought." Her smile was the mirror of her soul, and it knocked the breath out of Logan's body. She smiled, and as if she couldn't get enough of saying the words, she softly confessed again, "I love you, darling."

The kiss they shared was more than a physical expression of their love; it was truly the bonding together of their innermost selves. It was a flowing together of their souls. For the longest time, they lay together on the bed, she on her side, his body molded to her curves, his arm over her. Each was lost in thought. Both of them lazily slipped into that hazy, dreamy world of supreme happiness.

Finally, Logan stirred, moving his hand to cup her breast. "We've got to get up, baby. Bert and Lethia are expecting us."

"Yeah," Danny murmured, "I guess we do." She stretched, thrusting her breast against his palm, loving the sensations created by the rubbing of her flesh against his. "If we're going to have the grand opening tomorrow night, we'll have to get back." Her voice lowered to a whisper as Logan's fingers began to touch her nipple. "But I can think of"—she gasped—"other things I would rather do."

"Other things?" Logan teased.

Danny flipped over, silencing him as her lips claimed his in a hot, fervent kiss and her hands began an exploration of his body, quickly making their way to the center of his sensitivity.

Danny eased her mouth away from his just far enough to say, "We'll go as soon as we've finished."

CHAPTER SIX

Much later that evening, Danella, bundled in a thick jacket, hunched her shoulders and jabbed her gloved hands deep into her pockets, moving closer to the warmth of the huge bonfire that blazed in front of the mill. She was glad that Logan had thought to stop by her house when they returned to Blaketon earlier. She had gotten her heavy jacket and had turned on the furnace. It was hard to believe that in such a short space of time a norther could blow in and replace the mild, hazy warmth with bitter coldness, but it had. By the time Danella and Logan arrived at the old mill, the temperature had dropped to a record low. Winter, settling in for a lengthy stay, had rudely ousted the gentle Indian summer.

Most of the decorating had been completed with only Bert and Logan staying to work after the early winter darkness had settled on the small community. As soon as they checked the last batch of wires that had been strung, they, too, would be ready to go. Stooping over, Danella grabbed several of the blankets that were lying near the fire and stretched them out, making herself a thick pallet. Wrapping another one around her legs and feet, she huddled near the flames; then, growing drowsy, she lay down, placing an odd jacket or two under her head as a pillow and gazing at the brilliant blaze that burst into the air. Higher and higher the flames danced, graceful, vivid splinters of scorching light. Softly and tenderly they played across her face, coloring her cheeks rosy and shading her eyes, giving them a secretive appearance.

Foremost on her mind and shining across her countenance was the wonder of her love for Logan. She marveled that it had taken her twenty-nine years to fall in love—twenty-nine years before she ever uttered "I love you" to a man. How ironic that the man should be Logan, the man whom she had hated for the past five years. And even more perplexing was the fact that she now loved him with an even greater intensity than she had hated him. And she wasn't sure of the status of their relationship.

Although she had to concede that he was an arrogant and determined man, one who could be unscrupulous if he chose to be, she would also have to admit that Logan was one of the most gentle people she'd ever met. She smiled, thinking how much of a teddy bear he could be—big, lovable, huggable. But at the same time she knew that if he was crossed, he would exhibit all the qualities of a grizzly.

His loving her wouldn't mean that she could manipulate him any more than she would let him control her actions. He would continue to be his own person, just as she would want to be her own. And with both of them being assertive and aggressive, Danella could foresee stormy sailing ahead. But she always envisioned their being in the same boat. There would be many things they wouldn't see eye to eye on. Tempers would

143

flare and there would be disagreements. But she remembered what Logan had said to her when he was telling her about Alma. Love would subdue the most violent; it would strengthen the weakest. It was the healing balm! With it they could soothe away all the irritants that would try to destroy their marriage.

Hearing the soft thud of feet and the low drone of voices, Danella stirred from her ruminations and sat up, draping an extra coat over her shoulders. She watched as Bert and Logan emerged from the shadows, appearing first as shapes, then more clearly. They dropped their equipment in the bed of Bert's truck as they passed by, Logan quickly moving toward Danella and the warm comfort of the fire, Bert toward the mill to turn off the central switch that controlled the lighting.

Squatting beside Danella, Logan splayed his hands over the fire, letting the flames dispell the chill. His eyes were watering, and his nose and cheeks were flushed a bright pink. Reaching up, he pulled his knit cap lower, covering his numbed ears.

"As always," he told Danella with a cocky grin, "you look comfy." He reached out and tapped the tip of her nose with a gloved finger. "Snug as a bug in a rug."

Danella had no time to make a cute retort, because Bert called out from the mill at about that time, and Logan answered. As the two men continued their discussion Danella's eyes hungrily scanned Logan's rugged visage, which had been given a carved look by the wintry cold, and she craved him. In just a matter of hours she had become totally wanton in her desires, unleashing a passion that she had never imagined she possessed—a passion that had been dammed up in her for a lifetime. She knew that when Logan touched her, she would welcome him with reckless abandon. Rather than her having been sated from lovemaking, she had been inflamed, desiring more, needing more.

But still she had a secret fear, one that tore her apart. Logan had played the field for so many years now, probably indulging in casual, friendly sex with half the attractive women he met, that she wondered if he would be able to settle down with one woman. She feared that he wouldn't. She wondered if she was a mere infatuation after all. Had his attraction been for the unobtainable rather than for her? Had this been nothing more than a passionate conquest? Would he find someone else when he went on his next business trip?

Shutting off the lights, Bert walked out of the mill and approached the fire, holding his hands out. "Well, folks, I'm headin' for the house. I'm cold to the bone, tired, and hungry."

"Yeah," Logan agreed, lowering a hand to help Danella to her feet, "we've got to be going too." His eyes swept over the blankets and the assorted jackets that were scattered around. "What do you want us to do with these?"

"Put 'em in the bed of the truck," Bert replied, "and I'll make sure this fire is out."

After Bert had driven away, Logan and Danella stood just a moment longer, lingering in the moonlit forest, hating to leave the Christmas beauty behind. So pure and untouched, Danella thought. So peaceful and serene. Then she felt Logan move closer behind her, and she felt his hands as they closed over her shoulders, pulling her against the security of his chest. When he spoke, she felt his warm breath on her neck.

"It's so pretty, it's hard to leave."

Danella nodded, remembering the awe she had felt when the lights were first switched on. The clear, sparkling lights, glowing a pristine white, glittered like

145

snowflakes in all the trees, bringing to life the brightly colored flowers that clustered around the bases of the trees, outlining the trail. Huge bushes glistened with gold berries, others with red berries. The holly and the poinsettias. The white lights shimmering on everything produced one of the most beautiful sights Danella had ever seen.

Then she thought about the chapel. A small white frame church with a steeple that pierced the sky, reaching into heaven, directly channeling some of its glory to earth. She would never forget the golden beauty of the sun's rays as they streamed through the stained-glass window in the front of the church, radiating a reverential aura throughout the building. Nor would she soon forget the soft music that poured from the organ as Lethia's fingers expertly caressed the keys.

Without thinking, Danny whispered to Logan, "The chapel would be an ideal setting for a wedding." When his clasp tightened on her shoulders, and he pulled her closer against his chest, she murmured. "What do you think?"

Logan smiled lazily. "I think so, too, Danella Jones." He turned her around in his arms and his lips touched her nose. "Now I think it's time for you and me to go home and go to bed. You're so, cold you're shaking."

"No, I'm not cold."

Even through the many layers of her clothing, Danella could feel the fire of his touch, which, like kindling, ignited the smoldering embers of passion. The flames leaped with such a force that she pressed closer to him, wishing they could merge into one. She could hardly endure the pain of her wanting.

"I'm burning up. I'm on fire for you." Her hands slid up to his face, and cupping his cheeks, she guided his mouth to hers. "Kiss me, darling."

146

His lips touched hers lightly, and he breathed his answer into her mouth. "Gladly, my darling. All my touches, all my love, belong to you." Then his embrace tightened, and they held each other as they kissed with a wild abandon.

The winter's cold couldn't douse the fire that burned within them; it couldn't deter their wanting. Oblivious to the elements, oblivious to their surroundings, they let their kisses deepen until they were weak with desire, until they were consumed with their cravings. Finally, Logan tenderly pushed away. He shook his head and smiled weakly.

"Let's go home, darling. Although this is the time for making love, it's definitely not the place."

"Then home it is," she murmured, letting him guide her to the car, "because I'm hungry, absolutely starved, for more than this."

As Logan revved the engine he cast her a wicked glance. "Could it be that I've created a monster?"

She cast him a most provocative glance. "Just a woman. One who has an insatiable appetite for love."

"Just for love?" he prompted.

"Just for *your* love." The words softly fled her lips, setting Logan ablaze with the same desire that ravaged her slender form.

"Then I'd better get you home, woman, so I can attend to your needs."

He turned the car around and headed down the narrow road. After the heater warmed the interior, Danella took off her gloves and squirmed closer to Logan, locking her hands over his shoulder. Reaching up, Logan caught one of her hands and guided it to his mouth, raining small kisses over the moist softness of her palm. The quicksilver motions made Danny's stomach churn, and when his tongue began a gentle flickering motion that utterly stimulated all her nerve endings, she gasped. Automatically she placed her other hand over her stomach. She didn't think she could endure the sweet torment any longer. Logan had created a hunger in her so great that she couldn't think straight; she didn't want to think straight. She just wanted to share passion's pleasure with him.

When they arrived at the house, Logan got his athletic bag and carried it to Danella's bedroom. Then they headed for the bathroom, stripping as they walked, leaving a trail of clothes. Jackets thrown over chairs. Shirts over the end of the bed. Shoes and socks on the floor. Together they stood in the four-legged bathtub under the hot shower, letting the warmth of the water slowly drive the cold from their bones. The warmth of the water rekindled the fire in their souls.

Taking the washcloth, Logan lathered it, smiling as he lifted the plastic dispenser of baby soap. "I told you that I was going to take care of my baby, and so I am. First of all, I'm going to bathe you."

Lifting his hand, he began to wash Danella's face, careful to keep the soap out of her eyes, lightly touching her cheeks, her forehead, her chin. With the rag draped over his palm, he brushed his hand over the arched column of her neck. He cleaned her ears, probing with his fingers into every nook and around each curve. As slowly, as fastidiously he rinsed her.

"No one's ever bathed me like that." Her body tingled with exquisite joy, and her voice was thick and husky.

"And nobody else had better ever do it," he growled, sweeping his washcloth-covered palm over her collarbone, the ends of the terry cloth tantalizing Danella's breasts.

Logan took great delight in her heightened breathing and her trembling. He smiled when she closed her eyes and flung her head back in absolute abandonment. His palm slowly, evocatively, inched down over the wet smoothness of her breasts, every stroke igniting a new fire of excitement in her body that led directly to her lower stomach. He deliberately dropped the washcloth, leaned over, and picked up the dispenser. Taking his time, he filled his palms with the thick soap and rubbed his hands together. Then with baby-soft touches he sensually applied the lotion to her breasts. His touch was a silky caress that Danella could hardly stand. He was surely driving her out of her mind.

His fingers rolled her nipples; his hands slid under and over. Every movement evoked her total response. Following the love commands, Danella threw her shoulders back, thrusting her breasts forward, faintly moaning her pleasure.

"And now to rinse you," Logan said, his voice thick and guttural.

He moved aside, exposing her to the full spray of the shower, and he watched as the clear, warm water cascaded over her body, the suds tumbling into the bathtub and pooling around her feet before whirling down the drain. When her skin glistened clean in the muted glow of the newly wired antique light fixture, she looked at him with her love-glazed eyes and whimpered. "Is this all?"

"No, my darling. Now I'll dry you."

His tongue gently lapped the water droplets from each breast, and each flick was like an electrical jolt, shocking Danella into passionate oblivion. Racked with this erotic torment, her soft moan turned to a husky groan; she was unable to suppress the love sound. Then his mouth closed around one of the hardened tips, and he gently suckled.

"Logan," she whispered. "Oh, God, Logan, I don't think I can stand much more. Don't—" The gentle tug of his mouth on her breast switched on the current of passion that flashed through her. "—don't dry me off," she begged, her voice teary with uncontrolled wanting. "I . . . don't . . . I don't think I can stand it."

"Just a little longer," he groaned, the words almost incoherent as he greedily indulged in tasting her body, his warm breath spraying across her breast, his tongue tantalizing the peak.

Danella's hands automatically wove through his sandy hair, her fingers digging into his scalp as the tender sucking became a more urgent tugging. When she thought she was crazy with wanting, when she thought she would faint from her yearning, Logan moved his head, but the reprieve was short-lived. His hot, moist mouth trailed fire to the other breast. Now his tongue began another tender foray, making light, circular motions around the taut crest.

Then came the final attack. She felt his hand stroking her inner thighs; she felt those fingers touch the point of her greatest sensitivity. She shuddered, and her fingers clenched Logan's hair. "Logan." The coarse plea escaped her dry lips. "Please, Logan. Take me now." She couldn't stand any more of the torment. He had to bring their lovemaking to its natural conclusion. He had to take her before her wanting destroyed her.

Finally taking mercy on her, unable to stand more himself, Logan stepped out of the tub and held her hand as she climbed out, water dripping from both of them onto the bath mat. Grabbing the large towel from the rack, he carefully sponged her dry, each touch as evocative as her bath. With whispered words of love, he guided her across the hall into her bedroom, not switching on a light, letting the soft glow from the

150

bathroom filter into the room. He turned the covers down, and they climbed into bed together, their arms and legs instantly interlocking as they once again raced toward fulfillment.

Logan's hands, his mouth, and his tongue joined in the sweet battle of love, rekindling the blaze, sure of victory. His fingers brushed over her breasts, down her stomach, and around her navel, and her arms tightened around his neck as she pressed her body closer to his. She arched until she felt the crisp hair of his chest against her nipples; she moved her hips until she felt the firm hardness of his arousal.

"When, baby?" His husky voice sent shivers of delight through her. His fingers drew erotic designs on her stomach, on her thighs.

Danella's legs opened, and she moaned her satisfaction. "Now, Logan. Right now."

He lowered his body over hers, and she wrapped her arms and legs more tightly around him, penning their bodies together. Gently he slipped into the cradle of her love. Clinging to him as if she were drowning and he were her only lifeline, she gave herself to him in frenzied abandon, casting years of inhibition away. Logan, allowing himself to flow in the urgent current of her arousal, claimed her with the same force, making sure she reached the very pinnacle of ecstasy, reveling in her inarticulate cries of joy, then joining her. As before, they lay together, a tangle of arms and legs, softly exchanging endearments, sweet kisses, and gentle touches.

Slowly they came down from their height, carefully bringing their gift of pleasure and fulfillment with them. Never had Danella felt so complete, so whole. Never had she felt this serene and happy. For a long time they lay in silence, each lost in thought. Finally, Logan rolled over and switched on the light, smiling into

151

Danella's big, blinking eyes. "I think if you don't mind, I could use some nutritional sustenance now."

Laughing softly, enjoying anything they did together, Danella donned her robe and slippers and went into the kitchen to prepare them a snack. "Anything particular you want?" she called, filling the coffee pot with grounds and water, placing it on the warmer, and setting the timer.

By the time she opened the refrigerator and took a quick inventory, he was standing behind her. Dressed in jeans and an unbuttoned blue shirt, he peered over her shoulder. Then he reached around and picked up the ham. "Ham sandwiches or omelets," he said, carrying the platter to the counter.

"Omelets," Danella declared with relish, lifting the egg carton and following Logan across the kitchen.

She opened the cabinet and reached for a mixing bowl, and while Logan gathered and chopped the ingredients, she whipped the eggs. As they cooked and later as they ate, seated around the small breakfast table in the kitchen, they talked easily, the conversation sweeping in many directions, from likes and dislikes in food to pros and cons in politics. After they cleaned up the kitchen, Danella hung the dishrag on the rack to dry. Then she turned to Logan, the exhaustion of the day catching up with her. Yawning deeply, she lifted her hand and covered her mouth.

"And now, my sweet"—Logan grinned at her, reaching up to rub his finger across the bump on his nose—"we'll watch a little television; then it'll be time for me to tuck you in bed."

Danella's face colored; her lips moved into a beautiful smile that reflected her happiness.

"I don't want to watch television. Just tuck me in bed."

"Danny girl, don't do this to me. I've got to go, and you're making it hard on me."

"You've . . . got . . . to . . . go!" The words, spoken so slowly and so softly were not a question. They were shocked surprise. "I . . ." She licked her lips. ". . . I thought you were going to spend the night with me."

"I . . . I had thought about it," he admitted reluctantly. Danella stared at him incredulously, and his heart broke at the disappointment that shimmered in her eyes. "But on second thought, I don't think it would be wise, sweetheart."

"Why not?" She couldn't believe that he was leaving her like this.

A tender smile tugged his lips at the corner. "For one thing, sweet, you still live in Blaketon, and you still have extremely nosy neighbors. At this point your reputation is at stake."

"I don't care about my reputation," Danny cried indignantly. That wasn't reason enough for his not staying with her. "What you and I do is our concern."

"True," he agreed in a low, calm voice, his hands automatically settling on his hips. "But when what you and I do affects Blaketon Pharmaceuticals, when it affects our work—in particular *your* work—we must make certain concessions."

"We could spend the rest of the weekend together at your place."

Danella's suggestion touched Logan's heart, and while one of his major concerns was her reputation in the community, there were other concerns—questions that plagued him, uncertainties that haunted him. He just shook his head, not trusting himself to speak. Where this woman was concerned, he was vulnerability personified, and he would easily give in to her pleas. Without looking at her, he walked through the house to pick up his scattered clothes. Danella followed and stood framed in the doorway to her bedroom, watching as he folded his soiled clothes, meticulously placing

153

them in a small plastic clothes bag that he carried in his athletic satchel.

She finally asked, "What's wrong, Logan? Have I done something wrong?"

He gave the zipper a yank, the metallic cadence echoing through the otherwise silent room.

"Was it . . . was it nothing more than getting me to bed?"

Logan's blue eyes lifted, and they were pools of misery. "No, love, don't ever think that." His fingers closed around the handles of the satchel and he gave it a jerk or two before he set it down on the bed. "It's a matter of loving you and doing the right thing by you."

"And leaving me is loving me? Leaving me is the right thing?"

"Believe me, Danny, I'm making the hardest decision that I've ever made in my life, and I'm making the decision that will be best for both of us."

"In what way?" Danella demanded. She pushed herself away from the door and walked into the room, not stopping until she stood at the end of the bed.

Logan dropped the satchel and walked around the bed, letting his blue eyes intimately caress Danella. Because he loved her, because his soul was attuned to hers, he saw beneath the cool exterior. He saw the uncertainty that raged and billowed inside her—the same uncertainty that assailed him. He moved closer to her until they nearly touched. He lifted his hands and cupped her sweet face.

"I love you." His lips touched hers softly and tentatively. Without leaving the sweetness of her lips, he whispered into her mouth. "I love you with all my heart, sweetheart, but I think you need some breathing space."

"No," she answered sharply. Already she feared losing him. "I'm breathing okay without any space. I like it just like this."

"I love it like this too. But I don't want to rush you too much. I want to give you time to really make your own decision." Danella shook her head, and Logan said, "Even if you don't think it's right, I do."

Danny felt as if a sharp object had pierced her heart; the pain was excruciating. "Why?" She could hardly utter the word because she couldn't understand the feelings that were assailing her. Logan had been pushing her, and it was he who had suggested love and marriage. And now he seemed to be backing off. She couldn't understand. "Why, Logan?"

"Danny girl"—carefully he chose his words, hoping, praying, that he could express his feelings to her—"it's more than our saying we love one another; it's more than our accepting each other's love. It's more like accepting facts. I'm the only man you've ever slept with. I'm afraid you don't know the difference between sexual attraction and love."

Certain of her love, certain of her heart, Danella didn't understand his argument. She felt as if he were purposely trying to hurt her. She jerked her face away from his hand and backed up a step, putting some distance between them. "Are you saying that you don't want to marry me because I'm an inexperienced lover?" Had it not been as good for him as it had for her? Had she disappointed him?

"No," he told her, "that's not what I mean. I just didn't know that you were a virgin."

Her indignation grew. "And that makes a difference? You could love me and marry me if I hadn't been a virgin." Her eyes were dark and cloudy with confusion.

Things were getting out of hand, and Logan wasn't quite sure how to handle them. He had never been up

155

against this before. "No, Danny, I think it was wonderful. Being your first lover makes me happier than anything else, but I'm also wise enough to know I can't rush you now. You're basking in the afterglow of love and romance. Right now I'm just an extension of your romantic fantasies. You need time to think things through."

"How little you know about me," she murmured.

"Let's take it slower, darling. Give ourselves time— time for you to know whether its love or infatuation." The soft words continued to bombard her ears. "Let's just go together for a while, Danny. No affair. No marriage. No commitment. No strings attached. Give yourself time."

No strings attached! Dear Lord! She wished it were only a string that held them together. She could sever that easily enough. But she was bound to him by something so strong that she could never break it. She moved away from him, lowering her head, absently running her index finger over the bedspread piping.

"I wish it were just a matter of a string, Logan, but it's not. It's a matter of the heart." She raised her eyes and stared at him. "For what it's worth, you've won my heart." The words whispered across the distance between them. "You could never have had my body without first having my heart." She paused for only a moment before she said, "Perhaps it hasn't meant as much to you, Logan. Maybe you think the only thing binding us together is sexual compatibility. If so, I agree with you: It's time for you to go."

"Danny," Logan said, his heart constricting with pain, "oh, Danny girl, you're deliberately misunderstanding me."

She shook her head, her voice still soft. "I'm not a girl, Logan. I'm a woman. A woman in every sense of the word."

He nodded. "Yes. A woman . . . in every sense . . .

of the . . . word." He paused, his blue eyes sweeping over her face. Again he saw the vulnerability of the woman he loved; he saw the fears and the uncertainties that were haunting her. He walked to where she stood and took her in his arms, kissing her face, kissing her tears away. "To hell with logistics," he muttered. "I can't stand any more of this. I love you to distraction, Danella Jones, and I'm not going to leave you." His lips touched hers in a deep, warm kiss, a kiss that reaffirmed his love, a kiss that reassured her confused, bruised soul. Eventually he said, "But I'm not going to spend the night here. We'll spend tomorrow together at the farm."

"Your parents' place?"

"Yes." Logan didn't lift his lips from her ears. He delighted in feeling her shiver in his arms. "We'll call and let Mom know we're coming for Sunday dinner." He chuckled. "She'll be so excited, she won't know which way to turn first." His breath was warm and moist, touching her cheeks and her temples, blowing in her ear. "She'll get on the phone and call Janet, and the three Windhams will come too." He lowered his voice mischievously. "And you can spend all day playing games with Tommy."

"How long will it take us to get there?"

"About four hours." Logan lifted his arm and, looking over Danny's shoulder, said, "If we leave now, we'll make it by one o'clock."

Danny chuckled. "Are you sure your mom won't mind our coming in at one o'clock in the morning?"

"Not at all," Logan retorted, pushing her out of his arms. "I'll call while you get dressed." The firm lips quirked into his sensual, beautiful grin, the key to which unlocked the door of happiness in Danny's soul. "They might give me some lip if it were just me driving up. But when they find out that I'm bringing you with me, they'll be delighted." He walked around the bed to

157

the nightstand and picked up the telephone receiver. "And tomorrow we'll leave early enough to arrive back in Blaketon in time for a buggy ride through Christmas Tree Forest. Then I'll bring you home, tell you a bedtime story, and tuck you into bed."

CHAPTER SEVEN

Parking close to Chandler's Wharf and turning off the ignition, Danella buttoned the front of her coat, tied a scarf around her head, and slipped on her gloves. After she dropped her keys into her purse, she paused a moment to look at the Christmas decorations and the people who were scurrying around, their arms loaded with packages. It was hard to believe that it was one week until Christmas, but it was, and she and Logan were going to spend the holiday together at her home. Smiling at the thought of introducing Logan to her parents, she tucked her purse under her arm, opened the door, and stepped into the December cold. Lowering her head against the blistering wind, she hurried toward Logan's office, fighting the elements and the Christmas shoppers.

At any other time she would have been caught up in the nostalgic beauty of the wharf and the yuletide spirit herself, but today as she moved down the cobblestoned alleyways and wooden sidewalks she didn't see the magic of the recreated seaport of the 1880's. Unnoticed were the trim white picket fences, the renovated houses turned businesses, the barrels and the rustic wagons that lined the wharfs. As she hunched her shoulders against the icy blasts of wind, she anticipated her coming weekend with Logan; she anticipated the coming holidays.

When she reached Warehouse E, she pushed through the heavy door, glad for the immediate warmth of the primitive interior. While she walked through the newest renovation at Chandler's Wharf, she stripped her scarf and gloves off, stuffing them into her coat pockets. Stopping for just a second, she looked at her reflection in one of the windows, hastily finger-combing her hair. Then she was shoving the door open and entering Logan's office.

"Good morning, Justine."

Justine Preston, Logan's secretary, looked up from her desk and smiled. "Good morning, Danella. How are you this wonderful Friday morning?" She reached up and patted the vibrant red curls that framed her face.

"Doing great. How about yourself?" Danny asked, lingering for just a moment to indulge in friendly chitchat. After they had conversed for a while, Danny asked, "Is Logan here?"

"Sure is," Justine answered. "I think he lives here these days. He's here when I leave in the afternoon; he's here when I arrive in the morning. He's—" The ringing of the telephone interrupted her spiel. Reaching for the receiver, she said, "Go on in. He's expecting you."

Then Danella was standing inside Logan's studio-office, leaning against the closed door, staring across the spacious, sun-filled room. She had liked the room from the moment she had first laid eyes on it. It was simple but elegant, tasteful yet functional. And it was totally Logan. At the far end of the room was Logan's desk;

across from that was his drafting table. At the near end was a sofa, occasional chairs, and the tables, which gave it a comfortable look.

Today, however, Danella wasn't thinking about the room or its decor. She was staring at the man whom she loved more than life itself. He was sitting at his drafting table, pen in hand, sketching. His elbow was propped on the desktop, and his head was in his hand.

He heard the door open but he didn't look up. Rather, he said, "Thank God, Justine! You've arrived in just the nick of time. I'm finished, and I do mean finished." He sighed. "Call Clark and let him know that I've got his layouts ready." He moved his elbow, running his fingers around the collar of the white shirt that peeked out of the rounded neckline of his gray pullover sweater. "See what he wants me to do with them, and if there's any more coffee, would you pour me a cup, please?"

Smiling but not answering, Danella slipped out of her coat and hung it on the coat tree. As she walked farther into the office, she laid her purse on the coffee table in front of the sofa and glanced at the bar, noticing the empty coffee pot. She didn't stop walking until she reached Logan. Lifting her hands, she placed them on his shoulders.

"There's no coffee, but I've been told that I'm a pretty good masseuse. Until we can get the caffeine, perhaps this will do." She began to massage him, her fingers firmly gripping the tired, tense muscles.

"Danny!"

His pen dropped with a dull thud, rolling to the edge of the table, falling unheeded to the floor. Logan spun around on his chair and stood immediately. His eyes swept over her: the pleated skirt in burgundy, mauve, and black plaid; the mauve blouse, the burgundy sweater-vest, the black high-heeled boots. When he looked into her face, Danella could see the admiration gleaming in the depths of his lovely blue eyes. She could see the eager welcome.

"I didn't think you'd get here until this afternoon."

Moving into the circle of his arms, she said, "I couldn't think straight at the office anymore. Television cameras, cameramen, crewmen, and reporters everywhere." She shook her head. "I couldn't get anything done, so I decided to come early."

"Wow! What an ego deflater," Logan protested. "Your coming early had nothing to do with your wanting to see me."

Contentedly, Danella rested against the warm contours of his body. "Well," she said, "maybe just a little teeny tiny bit."

Logan's hand slid down her back, and he playfully swatted her buttocks, but he quickly forgot that he was meting out punishment, and his touch became a gentle caress.

"Did Lethia come with you?"

Danny shook her head. "They were still interviewing her when I left, but she promised that she'd be here by three o'clock sharp." Danella ran her hands up his chest, pressing her palms against the soft angora wool. "Since you're fresh out of coffee, Mr. Spencer, how about letting me take you to get a cup?"

Logan pulled them together. "That's not a bad proposition, Ms. Jones," he said, his lips leisurely mapping out the delicate terrain of her face. "But I've got a better one in mind." His lips touched hers in butterfly kisses, warm, fluttering, tantalizing.

"What's that, Mr. Spencer?"

"How about my taking you out to lunch? I'm starved. I've been working since about six this morning, and I haven't taken time to eat." His lips found hers, stopping further discussion as he kissed her thoroughly. When he finally ended the kiss, he murmured, "Well, Ms. Jones, what do you think?"

162

"Hmmm," Danella said, "I think I like this much better than lunch." Her hands glided around his neck, and her fingers twined in the waving locks that teased his shirt collar. "I think there are other things I would rather do than eat."

"A woman after my own heart," Logan sighed happily.

"And your body," Danella whispered, her hands sliding under the sweater.

She was delighted when Logan shivered and said huskily, "If you want my body, woman, I'll give it you willingly. Anytime, anyplace." Then he sealed her lips with a soft snarl of pleasure and asked, "Did you come to stay through the weekend?"

"I did," Danny replied, showering kisses around his mouth and across his jaw.

"Good. I have a special surprise for you." The words were lost as he twisted his head to reclaim her lips with his, and it was a long time before he explained. "One of my clients gave me and my favorite girl—"

" 'Favorite girl,' " Danella teasingly interrupted.

"Favorite and only girl," Logan amended. "Well, anyway, he gave me tickets for a special Christmas production at the Cobblestone Dinner Theater tomorrow evening."

Danella giggled, her fingers sliding between the buttons of his shirt to touch the warmth of his chest. "Shall I tell you what I've made reservations for, Logan Spencer?"

She felt his lips touch hers like the whisper of his words. "No, my darling, I'll just let you show me. I like the element of surprise. I enjoy anticipating." His lips lightly pressed against hers; then they gently covered hers in a hot, demanding kiss that sent new spirals of ecstasy through Danny.

"I'd suggest that if you're going to behave in this manner, you leave the office," Justine teasingly called from the door. "You're shocking my modesty." When Logan lifted his head and threw her a mocking grin, she added dryly, "Not to mention what you're doing to my body temperature."

"We're just about to leave, Justine," Logan said. "Danny's taking me to lunch." Then, as he helped a red-faced Danella into her coat, he gave Justine a few last-minute instructions. Darting back to his desk, he picked up a thin notebook and waved it through the air, saying, "And this, Danny Jones, is what you came for. One of the best campaigns I've planned to date. I know you and Horace will be proud of it. And Lethia too." There was a breathless pause of anticipation; then a small smile played on his lips. "I discussed the idea with her, but I can hardly wait to see what she thinks of the end result."

The words stung Danny, but she didn't give way to her disappointment. She wondered if she would ever conquer the burning resentment she felt at the camaraderie Lethia and Logan shared. Danny could understand Logan's respect for Lethia's opinion, but at the same time she wondered when hers would mean as much to him. As quickly as the nagging thought occurred to her, though, Danella dismissed it. Once and for all she had ousted the memory of Jackie Wesson from between them, and she was not about to replace it with jealousy for Lethia Blake.

Unconscious of the impact of his words on Danella, Logan laid the notebook down. "We'll go over this after lunch. Right now, let's go get some food."

Logan and Danella left the warehouse and strolled through Chandler's Wharf, headed for Michael O'Grady's at the Cotton Exchange. In the dimly lit Irish pub, they talked and ate lunch.

"Of course Mom was disappointed that we weren't going to spend Christmas with her, but she's so happy that you're taking me home to meet your family that she promptly forgave us," Logan said, laying his napkin on the table. "And she was excited about our spending the New Year's weekend with them. She said they might save our Christmas tree until then." He laughed quietly as he thought about his nephew. "Tommy will like that. Stretch the presents out over a week's period."

"Ummm," Danella said, swallowing her food. "I like that too." Her eyes were shining with anticipation. "The Christmas holidays will last longer this year than they ever have. And it'll mean more family than ever before, Logan." Her eyes twinkled with the undiluted joy that surged through her. "Can you imagine what it's going to be like when both our families get together?"

"I really haven't gotten that far, sweetheart," he softly replied. "Right now my fantasy includes only you and me."

Danella caught her breath when she saw the beautiful glint of love in Logan's eyes. Logan laughed softly, reaching across the table to capture her hand in his. "Danny, I love you." His grasp tightened, and he whispered a second time, "I love you, my darling."

"And I love you," she said, leaning over the tiny round table that barely separated them. Their lips touched, hinting at a kiss but sealing a promise of true love.

Afterward they leisurely strolled with the crowds through the Cotton Exchange, the intown shopping center that was housed in the restored old buildings on Wilmington's waterfront. Her mind totally on Logan and the coming yuletide holiday, Danny lost herself in the romance and flavor of the bygone era of the nineteenth century as they walked arm in arm through the brick walkways and enjoyed the antique furnishings and fixtures.

When they returned to Logan's office, Danella curled

165

up in a chair and Logan handed her the layouts. While she looked at them, he fixed a pot of coffee.

"Well, what do you think?" he asked after he'd given her time to look through them.

Danella didn't answer immediately; rather, she continued to flip through the layouts. After Logan had poured the coffee and set hers down on the table, she leaned forward, picked it up, and took that first swallow. Cradling the cup in both hands and continuing to balance the notebook in her lap, she looked at Logan, who had flopped down on the sofa. He kicked his legs straight out and locked his hands behind his head.

"I don't like it."

"You don't like it!" Logan couldn't believe his ears. He had worked too hard on this campaign for an outright rejection. This wasn't the reaction he had anticipated. "What don't you like about it? The fact that we're using a drawing of Lethia?"

Setting her cup on the table, Danella picked the notebook up, idly turning the plastic-covered pages. "That's one thing," she drawled.

"But Lethia doesn't mind. I wouldn't have done it without getting her permission first."

Danny felt a twinge of irritation when she heard Logan admit that he'd discussed the layout with Lethia rather than her. "I wish you had discussed this with me first," she said. "I could have voiced my objection before you put so much work into this." She lightly tapped her hands on the opened book. "This isn't Blaketon Pharmaceuticals, Logan."

"And if it's not Blaketon Pharmaceuticals, pray tell, who is it?"

Danella hesitated. She hated to give voice to her criticism, because she knew Logan would think she was being spiteful rather than objective. But she could be no less than honest with him.

"It's Lethia Blake."

Logan's eyes narrowed, and he smiled benignly, as if dealing with a temperamental child. "Danny, how many times must I tell you that you don't have to worry about your image. You're day is coming, so there's no need for you to feel this way about Lethia. You're going to get all the glory and credit for having salvaged the company."

"I'm not worried about my image or my day," she told him, striving to keep her voice even. "I'm not worried about glory or credit. I'm worried about the image we're projecting for the company that I'm establishing. And I don't want the company image to center on one individual, real or cartoon."

"Everyone has a logo, Danny," Logan pointed out. "And what better logo could Blaketon Pharmaceuticals have than Lethia Blake?"

"That's just it, Logan. It's *Blaketon* Pharmaceuticals," Danny calmly explained. "Blake Company failed. When Horace Warrington bought the company, we opened it under the name Blaketon Pharmaceuticals. We are now a part of the community rather than an extension of the Blake family."

Having worked long and hard hours trying to get all his projects tied up before Christmas, Logan was tired and irritated. He ran his hand through his hair in frustration.

"But the Blakes are Blaketon."

"No, Logan, that's where you're wrong. As an insider you can't see it, but as an outsider I can. The Blakes are not Blaketon. The Blakes may have been Blake Company, but they are not Blaketon Pharmaceuticals. From the first day of November, the Blakes absolved all responsibility for Blake Company. It's Horace Warrington's money and my expertise and leadership that's creating a new company: Blaketon Pharmaceuticals."

167

"And something that you have continually forgotten, overlooked, or discredited," Logan snapped, "is that you and Warrington both need my expertise in publicity."

"True," Danny concurred, "but—"

"Danny," Logan said, not allowing her to finish her statement, "I'm tired of your jealousy, and I'm tired of it's interfering with your professional judgment. This is immature and I don't like it. You have defied me from the beginning. Everything I suggest, you veto."

"I'll have you know I am not jealous, nor am I being immature," Danella flared. "You asked me what I thought about your campaign, and I, the manager of Blaketon Pharmaceuticals, told you. Now, if you'll just get off your high horse for a minute, you'd see the reasons why."

"I know why," Logan thundered, bounding to his feet and marching to the bar. He lifted the coffee pot and filled his cup again. "You're jealous as hell of Lethia Blake and have been ever since you took this position." He turned and looked at her. When he spoke again, the thunder was gone from his voice. Instead it was silky; it issued a challenge. "Where she's concerned, you're insecure. Deep down you're afraid she's going to steal some of your glory."

Danella's mouth fell open, and temporarily she was speechless. She couldn't believe that the man she loved, the man who professed to love her, could know so little about her. How could he make accusations like that? Finally she swallowed the knot of disappointment.

"I'm not afraid of Lethia, Logan," she admitted softly. "Although I am jealous." She saw smug satisfaction settle across his countenance. "But I'm not jealous in the sense that you're implying. I'm jealous because you and she share a working relationship that you and I haven't shared yet." Her faint smile held a touch of sadness. "We've shared our bed and our bodies, but we haven't shared that close bond of friendship that the two of you seem to share—a professional respect." Her voice dropped to an agonizing whisper. "And for that reason I am as jealous as hell of Lethia."

Logan set his cup down and walked to Danella. Taking her in his arms, he held her, pressing her head to his chest. "Baby, I didn't mean to lash out at you like that. I'm just tired. I've been working day and night to get everything finished before we leave, and now this. Your reaction has hit me cold. Believe me, your opinion does matter."

Neither spoke for a long moment as they held each other. Finally, Logan said, "Just trust me, Danny girl. I promise you my campaign will work. Just give it a chance."

Danny shook her head. "I can't, Logan, and I won't endorse this if you present it to the board. I'm going to insist that we make an immediate change in the direction of our publicity come January."

Logan's arms dropped. He stepped back and stared into her face.

"Ever since you and I first met, Danella, we've been at loggerheads. Talk about professional respect: I've never gotten that from you. You've never recognized my expertise in publicity." His hands rested on his hips. "Well, let me tell you something, baby: I know publicity, and I know we must capture the public's attention. And right now Lethia Blake is the best way."

"Not the best way," Danella contested, refusing to give ground. "The quickest, because we're appealing to people on an emotional level. And I don't want that, Logan. It may take longer my way, but I want to appeal to their intellect and their reason. And I think the board will agree with me. I think I've been there long enough for them to know that Blaketon Pharmaceuticals is my primary concern. I believe I can convince them."

169

Logan looked at her with incredulity. "You think I'm so narrow-minded and so inept that I would play only on the public's emotions?" His eyes blazed with his anger. "You"—he pointed his finger at her and hurled his words—"the managerial consultant—the person who saves floundering companies—are telling me how to do my business. You're telling me how to do publicity." Danella's mouth opened, but Logan didn't give her a chance to speak. "I want you to know, Danella Jones, that I've been in the business for many years, and I'm considered one of the best in the country. And I got where I am without any help or advice from you."

"I'm sorry, Logan," Danny murmured, extending her hand in a placating gesture. "I didn't mean for it to sound the way it did. I'm not faulting your expertise or knowledge. I'm just saying that I've got this gut feeling that the campaign you've planned isn't the one for Blaketon Pharmaceuticals." Her voice pleaded with him for understanding. "What it boils down to is the old versus the new. And I want a new image for a new company. I want to break away from the Blakes."

Ignoring her last comment, Logan whipped out, "So who do you want to represent the company, Danny? *You?*"

"No, not me, but we must project a credible image it must be a trustworthy image."

"My, God! Who could be better for this than Lethia? If anyone's trustworthy and credible, Lethia Blake is. She has Blaketon at heart, and she's the heart of Blaketon."

Knowing she was treading on thin ice, Danella said, "No, Logan, she doesn't have Blaketon at heart. Although you don't recognize it, you said it yourself the other day. At heart Lethia is concerned only with being a Blake."

Logan plunged his hand into his hip pocket and

170

walked to the small warehouse windows that lined the back wall of his studio-office. He looked at Chandler's Wharf, hustling and bustling with Christmas shoppers; he looked at the peaceful Cape Fear River.

"You're right, Danny, but you've got to admit that she has the ability to generate national interest, which in turn will be focused on Blaketon Pharmaceuticals."

Danny shook her head even though Logan wasn't looking at her. "Logan, please listen to me. Hear what I'm saying. If you weren't so close to this, you would see that Lethia Blake is hardly local interest, much less national."

Logan spun around. "The board doesn't agree with you on that. Just because you're insecure where she's concerned—"

Danny didn't let him finish his sentence before she came back with "Believe me, Logan, no one outside Blaketon is interested in Lethia Blake, and Blaketon alone is not large enough for this company to survive and grow on. And whether you believe it or not, my concern is the well-being and growth of Blaketon Pharmaceuticals, not the Blake name. The Blakes were not able to survive on their own popularity. Why should we try to build a national firm and reputation on one family that could not survive in its own community." Danella's voice was loud and authoritative. "We will build our company's credibility in Blaketon, the surrounding community, the state, and the nation in the same manner that it is being built throughout this country; not on one person, not on one local family, but on the product and service that we can deliver to the people."

"You haven't been able to see any of my plans and projections for looking at Lethia Blake, have you?" Logan walked across the room to stand at his drafting board and looked down at some sketches. His toneless words barely reached Danny, who now sat on the sofa.

171

"If you had, you would have noticed that I was capitalizing on the product and the service. You would have noticed that I was building a new image for a new company. I was just moving slower than you want to move." He picked up a pen and began to draw. "You seemed to agree that Lethia was the perfect spokesperson for the company."

"For this phase of our publicity, I did and I still do," Danny returned. "We're focusing attention on the Blake Mill, on the Blake House, and on Christmas Tree Forest, which is local history, and what better person to advertise than the historical persona herself. But I don't want our future campaigns to be planned around one person." Logan dropped the pen and turned to stare at her. "I mean it, Logan. I will not accept or approve of it, and if you insist on presenting it, I will do my best to influence the board to reject it."

"Horace liked it."

Anger surged through Danny. She resented Logan's treating her as if her position were a sinecure, as if she were of no consequence; she resented his going to Horace over her head. She resented his discussing his plans with Lethia first.

"You went over my head once before, Logan. I didn't appreciate it then, and I don't now. Horace delegated this job, this position, and this responsibility to me, and I will execute it as I see fit. Anytime he wants to replace me, he can. Until then, you come directly to me."

"Dear Lord, Danny," Logan exclaimed wearily, "I didn't go over your head. Before I could plan the campaign, I had to have Lethia's permission to use her as the caricature persona, and when I was in Atlanta, Horace just asked me how things were going, so I sketched out the idea to him." He shrugged and reached up to massage the back of his neck with his hand. "Nothing personal meant."

172

"So now you've presented the idea to me, and I don't like it, and I'm the opinion that counts the most."

"I think not," Logan replied. "Keeping a Blake on the payroll was one of the conditions of the takeover, but since then Lethia has earned her salt. She's more than a figurehead, so she's got some say in this."

"Very little," Danny retorted.

"But enough to sway the board," Logan said. "That's what you're afraid of, isn't it, Danny?"

"Yes, I'm afraid," she said softly. "I'm afraid of Lethia's opinion. I'm afraid that she's as biased as you are."

"And you're not," Logan mocked. Before either could say more, the intercom buzzed. Moving to his desk, Logan touched the button, and Justine's voice came through. "Lethia Blake to see you." Logan looked across the room at Danella, and when she nodded, he said, "Send her in."

Lethia was even more radiant than usual. Her eyes were dancing and her cheeks were glowing; her hair was elegantly styled, and her dark wool dress and creamy pearls enhanced her beauty. After she was seated with a cup of coffee in hand, Danella handed her the notebook of layouts. Both Danny and Logan watched with bated breath as she looked. Both waited for her reaction.

Finally, when she was through looking, Lethia looked up, first at Danny, then at Logan. She smiled. "You draw a pretty mean caricature, Logan. This one"—she tapped a long, vibrant red nail on one of the drawings—"is almost too real. Reminds me of myself when I get up in the morning. I must have been crazy to agree to this scheme of yours."

They laughed. Even Danny couldn't help grinning a little, and some of the tension evaporated from the room.

"What do you think?" Logan asked, sitting on the edge of the sofa, dangling his hands between his legs.

As if she felt the undercurrent of disagreement between Logan and Danny, Lethia hesitated to reply. "I would be a fool not to like it, Logan," she slowly admitted. "I enjoy being the center of attention, and I like being spokeswoman for Blake Company—" Hastily she amended, "I mean Blaketon Pharmaceuticals." She closed the book and she looked at Danella. "I have a feeling that you're unhappy, Danella. Is it my being the spokesperson?"

Danny shook her head. "No, I don't mind that. To the contrary, I feel that you should be the one to travel and to promote Blaketon Pharmaceuticals. You're good at it and you enjoy the limelight."

"But . . . ?" Lethia could tell there was a lot more that Danella had left unsaid.

Danny took a deep breath and looked Lethia squarely in the eyes. "But I don't think you should be the logo for Blaketon Pharmaceuticals." Lethia raised her brows in question, and Danny succinctly recounted the same reasons to Lethia that she had given Logan. "It's not you personally that I'm opposing," she concluded. "I'm opposing the idea of centering all our promotion on any one individual."

Lethia pursed her lips and nodded, finally saying, "I can understand your point, Danny. At the same time I can see the advantages of Logan's campaign. This would draw immediate local attention, which in turn might capture national interest. But," she added softly, "would this be the wisest move in the long run? Does Blaketon Pharmaceuticals want a logo that in time will hang like an albatross around its neck?" She paused, lifting a finger to her lips. "Like you, I must say I don't think so."

A satisfied smile curved Danny's lips, and she turned to glance at Logan, who hadn't joined in the conversation at all. He stood in front of the windows, again staring at the peaceful river. When he didn't turn, Danny stood and walked to the bar, setting her empty cup down.

"I'm not going to endorse this campaign if Logan presents it to the board," she said, her flat tone ringing with finality. "And I would appreciate it if you would support me with your vote and if you'd repeat what you just told me to the board."

"No," Lethia replied, much to Danny's surprise, "I don't think I'll be siding with either you or Logan on this one, and this is one vote from which I'll abstain." She stood, reaching for her coat.

"How can you keep silent when you feel the same way I do?" Danny demanded. "You know how the board feels about you. You know how much they respect your opinion, and you fully understand that your silence and abstention will sway their vote in favor of this."

"I'm not so sure that's the truth anymore, Danella. And if it is, it's time that you changed it. This is your little red wagon, and you must pull it. You, Logan, and the board are going to have to figure this one out." She smiled at the younger woman. "Now, if you and Logan will excuse me, I have some shopping to do while I'm in town. Then I'm off to dinner."

The sound of the closing door resounded through the room, finally giving way to the heavy silence. Danella looked at the clock; she looked at the heavy black hands. At the moment she felt all the old resentment and hatred for Lethia Blake festering in her heart, but she didn't have time to dwell on her own feelings. She had to think about Logan, who still stood at the window.

She knew he was hurt and angry, and she wanted to go to him. As his lover, she was the one to comfort him, to give him solace; but as the manager of Blaketon Pharmaceuticals, she was the one who had hurt him. At odds about what to do, she just stood there. Eventually, Logan turned, both hands in his pockets. Without looking at her, he walked to the coffee table and picked up the notebook. He turned, crossed over to his drafting board, and dropped it.

"I'll probably be working late this afternoon," he said, reaching into his pocket for his keys as he moved toward Danella. Flipping one off the ring, he handed it to her. "Here's the key. I'll be home later."

"Logan . . ."

Logan took Danella's hand in his, pressed the key into her palm, and gently closed her fingers. "Not right now, honey. I'd like to be by myself." When tears misted Danella's eyes, he added, "Please."

Too choked up to say anything, Danella nodded, leaned over, and picked up her purse. She opened it, dropped the key into one of the small compartments, and closed it. Then she slipped into her coat. As her fingers closed around the doorknob she said, "I'll cook supper for you."

"Don't," he replied. "I don't know what time I'll be home. I'm going to stay until I've finished what I'm working on now. I want to have everything tied up before Christmas."

"What about your dinner?"

"I'll send for something or get something on the way home."

"Don't stay late, Logan," Danella pleaded. "You're tired and you need your rest." She released the doorknob and turned to where he stood. Lifting a hand, she traced the lines of exhaustion around his eyes and the corners of his mouth. "Justine said you'd been working day and night, and you look it."

Logan smiled, his face marked with amused tolerance. "I'm going to have to get on that woman about gossiping."

Understanding her need for his reassuring touch, he

drew her closer to him. Then he realized that as much as she needed and wanted him, he needed and wanted her. At that very instant he was drawing strength from her. He turned his head, resting his cheek against her forehead, sighing deeply. For the longest time they stood, neither speaking, both savoring the sweetness of the moment.

"What time shall I expect you?"

"I'm not sure, honey. Probably pretty late. Why don't you go shopping and stop at the Treasure Chest for something to eat."

Danella's arms tightened, and she swallowed the tears that threatened. She couldn't stand Logan's withdrawing from her like this. She could hold back the tears, but she couldn't stop the pain of disappointment from racking her body. She couldn't dam the fear that ran rampant in her heart and soul. There was so much she wanted to say. There were questions she wanted answered. There were doubts she wanted assuaged. But this was not the time. . . .

She lifted her face to his, her lips soft and tremulous, her eyes luminous with her love. "Logan, I love you."

A sweet, tender smile touched his lips and colored his eyes. "I know, darling, and I love you."

"No . . . no matter what," she whispered. "No matter how long. I'll be waiting for you." The tears were so close, she could hardly blink or swallow them back any longer. Reaching up, she locked her hands around his neck and pressed herself to the warm closeness of his body. Tightly she held on for what seemed like an eternity and nestled her cheek against the softness of his sweater.

Then she slowly pushed herself out of his arms and left the room. Just before the tears began to run unchecked down her cheeks, just before she closed the door, she whispered, "I'll be waiting, darling."

Danella drove straight to Logan's condo, not even stopping for dinner. Once she was there, she unpacked her suitcase and changed clothes. As she hung up her skirt and blouse she wondered about the wisdom of her falling in love with Logan. Look how vulnerable it had left her. Just when she had let down every barrier that would separate her from Logan and his love, look what had happened. They disagreed on one of the most crucial points in their careers. And the disparity was so great that both had been hurt by the other's reaction. Was a professional difference of opinion going to sever the cords of their budding relationship?

Danella wandered through the house and thought about all the plans she and Logan had been making, the holiday fun they had been anticipating. As the hours slowly ticked by she tried a million things to take her mind off her worries. She tried to read the newspaper; she tried to watch television; she tried to read a novel; but nothing kept her interest long. How many times she walked to the phone to call him—how many times she picked up her purse and walked to the door—she couldn't count. But she did neither. She had told him she would wait, and she would wait. Finally, when hunger refused to be ignored any longer, she went into the kitchen and searched the pantry, coming up with a can of soup and a tin of crackers.

Exhausted from her anxiety and waiting, she took a bath, donned her new nightgown, and went to bed. She switched off all the lights except the small one beside the bed, and she lay there, waiting and watching and praying. A little after midnight she heard the front door open. She heard the soft footfalls, and her pulses began a sudden leap of excitement. She saw him in the doorway. Quickly she closed her eyes, a delightful shiver of desire running through her.

Logan's frame filled the doorway. He was exhausted, but he was relieved. He had made his decision. Thinking Danella was asleep and not wanting to awaken her, he quietly walked into the room, unbuttoning his shirt as he moved. As he unfastened his belt he stopped, bent over, and took off his shoes and socks. He kicked off his slacks. He was at the bed now, and he ran his hands beneath the elastic of his shorts, pushing them down his thighs and over his knees, and stepped out of them.

He switched off the lamp and lifted the covers, sliding into the bed, curling his body around hers. He sighed with pleasure as he drank in the comfort of her nearness. He draped his arm over her, his hand falling against her breast. He lay there for a few minutes, listening to her uneven breathing, feeling the quickening palpitations of her heart. He smiled and carefully lifted his arm. Then slowly he began to draw imaginary designs on Danella's back, moving from her shoulders to her waist to her buttocks.

She shivered as passion flowed through her; she luxuriated in his touch. His fingers magically turned her night into day, her sorrow into joy, her worry into the certainty of his love. When his whisper-soft touches moved to her inner thigh, Danella could stand the torment no longer.

When she gasped, he chuckled. "Playing possum on me, Danny Jones?"

She turned and giggled, "I was trying to play hard to get, but just one touch and I was yours for the taking. So I guess I must be playing possum."

His hands ran the delicate length of her body, and he murmured, "That's odd. You don't feel like a possum." His lips gently nipped the smooth contours of her face, the curves of her ears, the planes of her neck. "You

179

don't taste like a possum either. You taste warm and sweet. You taste like more."

"Definitely more," she whispered, her mouth touching his. "I taste like a woman in love," she whispered. "I feel like a woman who needs love." She began to touch him. "And you, my darling"—her fingers curled around him—"feel like the man who can fulfill all my needs. The only man," she added, her lips seeking his again.

"That I am," he promised, allowing her to capture his lips, "because I'm the man in love with you, and the man who needs your love."

At that moment love was what they both needed. True, there was much to talk about, disagreements to discuss, differences to be ironed out, but it was the time for loving not talking. It was the time for the spiritual and emotional healing that comes with love. Both of them needed it; both of them deserved it.

The next morning Danny slowly uncurled, lifted her hands above her head, and stretched her legs. She opened her eyes to the early sun that peeped through the drapes, and she turned her head on the thick, downy pillow, her gaze traveling the room, coming to rest on Logan's clothes, which lay in a trail from the door to the bed. A soft and loving smile touched her lips as she remembered his coming to her.

Then she realized what had awakened her. She smelled the coffee; she smelled the bacon and the toast. Jumping out of bed, she stepped on her nightgown, which she had discarded during the night, but she didn't stop for it. She grabbed her robe from the back of the rocker as she ran through the house, stopping in the kitchen door, gazing affectionately at Logan.

Looking up, Logan saw her and smiled. "Good morning, sleepyhead," he said as he opened the refrigerator and poured two glasses of orange juice.

Danella smiled at him, the innocence and purity of her love clearly in her eyes. "Good morning."

"How do you like your eggs?" he asked, putting the glasses on the table.

"Scrambled. Dry."

"Scrambled eggs, dry," he said gaily, pointing the spatula to the chair. "Pour yourself a cup of coffee, Ms. Jones, and have a seat. Your breakfast is just about ready."

As they ate, Logan kept up the cheerful flow of conversation, but he never once mentioned work. When the meal was over, the kitchen cleaned, and they were drinking their last cup of coffee, Logan still hadn't ventured the topic that was occupying most of Danella's thoughts. Finally curiosity overcame determination.

"Logan, what about the publicity?"

Logan grinned. "I wondered how long it would be before you asked."

"Now you know," she said. "So answer the question."

"Well, Ms. Jones, I thought about everything you said, and you almost had me convinced." His eyes sparkled with challenge. "Almost. But then I remembered that I'm one helluva publicity guy. I might go so far as to say I'm an expert. And I knew that I had mapped out a fantastic publicity chart no matter what you may think."

Danella took a swallow of coffee. "Even though you know that I'm going to oppose your layouts, you're going to present them to the board?"

Logan nodded. "I am." He chuckled. "And you may convince them to veto it, but I'm going to give it a try because I believe in it, Danny. I'm going to fight for it."

"How . . . how is this going to affect us?" Danny asked, drawing imaginary designs on the tablecloth.

181

"It shouldn't," he replied. "Unless we're too immature to handle the situation. We're just going to agree
to disagree about some things. We've had our first
professional disagreement, but that was a difference of
opinion between Logan Spencer, PR man, and Danella
Jones, manager of Blaketon Pharmaceuticals. We're not
going to let that interfere with our personal lives. It's
nothing that should affect our loving one another."

Danella grinned. "If I almost convinced you to change
your own publicity campaign, I'll bet I can convince the
board."

Logan chuckled contentedly. "I've come up against
some pretty tough opposition in my time, Danny Jones,
but I have to say you're the toughest." He leaned across
the table and tweaked her nose. "But I still think I'm
going to swing this one."

"What will you do if you don't?"

"That, dear heart, is why I worked so late tonight.
I've come up with an alternate plan that I shall submit
if the first one's not chosen. And if I don't come up with
anything you like, you'll just have to hire someone else
for publicity."

"That won't bother you?" Danella asked.

"Yes, it would bother me. I haven't lost too many
contracts in my career." Then he added on a lighter
note, "But losing this one would bother me even more
than usual, especially if the next guy you hire is young
and good-looking." He smiled at her and caught her
hand in his. "But let's shelve this until Monday morning.
This is our time, and I don't intend to share you with
anything or anyone. And nothing—" He paused, letting
his words sink in. "—and I mean nothing—is going to
mar our time together or come between us."

He stood, pulling Danny up with him and kissing her
gently on the lips. "I just may have a secret weapon to
use on you, Ms. Jones," he said. "Perhaps I'll try some

182

loving persuasion to pull you around to my way of thinking."

"I'm all for the loving persuasion," Danny whispered as they walked to the bedroom, "but I don't think it'll change my opinion about the publicity."

CHAPTER EIGHT

On Monday morning the small group that constituted the board of Blaketon Pharmaceuticals sat around the table in the conference room. All eyes were glued on Logan and the podium. Although Danella didn't agree with him, she felt proud of him as she listened to his presentation. He was confident and sure of himself, and he looked and sounded every inch the professional.

"So ladies and gentlemen," Logan concluded, smiling and nodding at the audience, "I'm open for questions and comments." Hardly had he uttered the words before he was being bombarded with questions. Eventually, when he had satisfied everyone's curiosity, he said, "If that's all, I'll turn this back over to Danella."

Danella rose and walked to the front of the room. "Thank you for your presentation and your patience, Logan." Her gaze flickered over each of the Blaketon employees seated around the table. "Are there any more questions?" She waited. When there weren't, she asked, "Are we ready to make a decision about Logan's package?" Again she waited while the members looked at their notes and pondered.

"I'm not sure I'm ready to vote, Danella," one of the men said. "I'd sorta like to bounce the ideas around awhile before we make a decision." The others murmured their assent.

Danella smiled and nodded. "That's a good suggestion, Norman." She looked at the other members, who were nodding their heads in approval. "And I see the rest of you agree."

Before the discussion could begin, Lethia spoke. "Danella, Logan, members of the board, I am going to ask to be excused." When several heads turned in her direction, she explained graciously, "I'm going to abstain from discussing and from voting on this issue."

"Oh, no, Lethia," one of the plant managers cried, his eyes resting on Danella as if he blamed her for Lethia's decision. "You have as much say in this as any one of us. And we're all waiting with bated breath to hear what you have to say."

Lethia stood, one hand lifting to touch the pearls that rested on her gray blouse. She smiled patronizingly at the little man. "Thank you, Mr. Morgan." Her soft voice so totally captivated the man, he was ignorant of her condescending tone. The smile she bestowed on the others seated around the table, however, was warm. "All of you must admit, I'm standing between the Devil and the deep blue sea." After the titter of laughter died down, she continued. "Ever since Danella and I discussed this package with Logan last Friday, I've been thinking about it, and I'm still of the same opinion I was on that day." She paused, then said, "I am too personally involved in this to be objective in my opinion; therefore, in the best interests of Blaketon Pharmaceuticals, I am leaving the vote to you." Lethia smiled at Danella first, at Logan next, then at the individual members. "Whatever your decision, I shall abide by it and support it wholeheartedly." After the small round of applause, Lethia gathered her purse and note pad and left the room.

"Before we go any further," Danella began, "I want to tell you a few things. Although I agree with many aspects of Logan's campaign, I do not want Lethia Blake—caricatured or otherwise—to be our logo." Then she repeated, adding, "Our spokesperson, yes; our logo, no." There, she had said it! she thought, looking defiantly at each one of the shocked faces. But Danella didn't stop for the hiked brows and the rounded eyes; she continued to talk. "My opinion in no way reflects personally on either Logan or Lethia, nor am I too personally involved to be objective. At the same time I am personally involved. As a Blaketonian and as a member of this company, I want Blaketon Pharmaceuticals to succeed. I want our success to ride on our greatest accomplishments: our service and our products."

Quickly and concisely Danella outlined her objections, going over them point by point. Then she said, "I know many of us are still undecided. Therefore I'd like to adjourn this meeting for one week to give us time to think things over."

Yesses were murmured and heads nodded in affirmation.

"Just remember, when you vote," Danella admonished, "your sole consideration should be whether you think this packet will promote our company in such a manner as to increase sales and put Blaketon Pharmaceuticals on a solid financial basis. *My* job and *your* job depend on the success of this branch in Blaketon; therefore emphasis should be based on company performance and the quality of our products and services." She smiled. "Adjourned to the Tin Bucket, where I'm treating you to lunch today."

The departure ritual was different that day. When one of the board members teased her by saying, "Is this an underhanded tactic to sway our vote?" all of them laughed together, and for the first time since she'd taken over Blaketon Pharmaceuticals, Danella felt as if she were one of the team, as if she were one of them. It was the first time they had willingly included her.

When Danny passed Lethia's office, she poked her head in. "The battle's over," she called. "You can join us for the victory march to the Tin Bucket if you wish."

Lethia pushed back her chair, smiling shrewdly at her employer. "How did things turn out?"

"Much better than I had expected."

"Oh?" Lethia mouthed the word more than she spoke it. "I take it Logan's packet was vetoed."

"No, we're not voting on that until next week, and it will take care of itself, Lethia." About that time Logan stepped up behind Danny and dropped his hands on her shoulders, peeking through the doorway too. But Danny continued to look at the older woman and made a candid confession. "On Friday, when you said you would not speak to the group, I almost hated you. I thought you were being spiteful." Her voice softened apologetically. "But now I understand, and I can see why Logan values your opinion. You knew the board wouldn't let us down, and you respected their judgment enough not to stoop to emotional blackmail." Turning her head and looking over her shoulder at Logan, Danny said, "No matter what decision they make, they will do what they honestly think is best for Blaketon Pharmaceuticals."

"And what if they vote for my package without any modifications?" Logan taunted lovingly.

"I hope not, Mr. Spencer," she quipped lightly. "But if they do, I shall give it my wholehearted support."

Pulling her out of the doorway and into the deserted hall, Logan said, "And speaking of wholehearted, Ms. Jones, I think it's time that we talked about a wholehearted commitment."

"If by now, Logan Spencer, you don't know that I'm wholeheartedly committed to you, you'll never know it."

"Being a Blaketonian at heart and having that small-town mentality," he said, "I think I'd like to make you legally mine. I'd like to be able to sleep with you wherever we are."

"I don't think even marriage affords that luxury," Danny dryly remarked just before Logan's mouth closed over hers.

Danella felt as if she were living her most beautiful fantasy. Christmas Tree Forest couldn't be real, she thought. It was a wonderland beyond description. The sparkling lights. The soft music. The bright array of flowers. She stood outside the chapel, thinking of all her friends who were sitting inside, waiting for her to be married. She watched her sisters as they marched one by one down the aisle. With a smile and a misty veil of tears, she thought of her parents sitting on one side; she thought of Logan's family sitting on the other. Then she heard the bridal chorus. She saw Logan. She began to move toward him.

Then she was at the altar and was looking into that face she loved so much. She heard the minister.

"Do you Danella Jones take this man—"

Candlelight Ecstasy Romances™

$1.95 each